To my FAN!
for the
and support

Praise for LACE & WHISKEY

"A fantastic, startling, near-perfect bit of reality. It could work as fiction, but then, who wouldn't. I look forward to Elston's next."
—*The Santa Ana Beacon*

"Elston outdoes himself with this one. LACE & WHISKEY is like a life sentence without plurals. The man knows where it's at. Where it's coming from. Where it's happening. The end will leave your lips dry, like a dead towel."
—Sax Woolrich, *Crime Waves*

"From the opening sentence: 'Never put a dollar on a horse named Immortality,' Elston shows that he's got a knack."
—Betty Benson, *The Palm*

"Nobody does the noir thriller better...His lean style and hard-edged characters—not exactly likable—but always compelling, provide a welcome return to the hard-bitten days of yore."
—*Santa Rita Times*

LACE & WHISKEY

From the Private Annals of Elston Brand
as told to

Jason Holscher

BRAND BOOKS

New York • London

Tokyo • Sweden • Milan

Copyright © 2010 by Jason Holscher

All rights reserved. No part of this book may be reproduced in any form or by any electronic or mechanical means, including information storage and retrieval systems, without permission in writing from the publisher, except by a reviewer who may quote brief passages in a review.

First Edition: April 2010

Manufactured in the United States of America

ISBN-13: 978-1452820934
ISBN-10: 1452820937

ically. Whatever it is — or was.
LACE & WHISKEY

Chapter One

Never put a dollar on a horse named Immortality.

It was the biggest all-aged race of the 1945 Flat season and I had all my rent money riding on a three-year old filly with good looks named Immortality to win.

I pounded on the rail and yelled my head off to push her home. "Come on, Immortality girl!"

Going into the final quarter-mile it was eyeball-to-eyeball between Immortality and a nice colt named Red Devil. Neither horse would give. They were inseparable up the straight, Immortality hugging the rail, Red Devil pressing upsides all the way, and they stayed locked together as they barreled round the bend and up the home stretch.

Something had to give...

...and what gave was Immortality's right foreleg.

Ten yards from the finish line, down she crashed, and crashing down with her were my hopes of paying off my assiduous and bulldogged bookie, Salvatore "Bedbug" Santucci.

Isn't that the way it always goes?

There you are cruising along, everything going according to Hoyle, and bang, the sky falls down on top of you and you're just another also-ran with bubble-gum dreams of hitting the big time someday.

I ripped up the losing ticket and shuffled out of the track. That's when I heard someone holler, "Brand!" and I knew it wasn't going to be good.

I looked over my shoulder and I didn't like what my optical nerves told me:

Jimmy "The Weasel" Triscaro and Leo "Leadpipe" Moceli—Bedbug Santucci's "collection agency"—were bearing down on me.

They drifted out of the crowd like a couple of bogeymen. Instinct alone must have told them I was there.

I turned and ran like a guy with three feet. At first I couldn't remember where I'd left my car, then I spotted her off to one side of the parking lot, a battered sky-blue 1940 Buick Electra (license plate PVT EYE) with one working headlamp and a NUKE HOLLYWOOD bumper sticker.

I jumped in and turned the key.

Click.

I turned it again.

Nothing.

She was as dead as the summer before last.

Leo and Jimmy were now pushing through the crowd like two overfed linebackers. Agonizing seconds, resembling entire lifetimes passed.

"C'mon, turn over. Come on," I urged, but that car of mine was as mean and stubborn as my ex-wife.

I looked up and saw Leo and Jimmy approaching the hood. They weren't in a hurry anymore and they weren't trying to sneak up on their quarry any longer. They had big grins on their big faces, like jackals that have just picked out the weakest antelope in the herd, and I'll give you one guess who that antelope turned out to be.

Leo the Leadpipe would have been in his element in the Roman Colosseum—and God help the lions. He had a face that looked like it caught on fire and someone beat it out with a log chain.

Jimmy the Weasel looked like a guy who couldn't scratch his own itch; a peanut M&M away from three-hundred pounds, and if you had to walk all the way around him you'd be tired.

Despite how ugly they were, or maybe because of it, Leo and Jimmy were very good at their job. If you welched on a bet with Bedbug Santucci, you could usually count on walking away from it with two or three missing digits.

I looked from Jimmy's face to Leo's face, and my own face must have whitened a little, just for a second though because I'd been expecting this for far too long to stay scared. Ever since I can remember, I'd been stealing from Peter to pay what I owe to Paul.

A plan came to mind. It was just as bad as all my other plans. I decided to scream until someone in the parking lot came to my rescue. To hell with dignity.

But then I changed my mind. What good would screaming do? This was southern California. No one was going to come to my rescue.

Truth was I was sick of dodging them, had a bellyful of trying to save my hide. I'd had it up to my neck, this business of keeping one step ahead of bill collectors, bookies, and pimps. So instead of screaming I pushed back the rim of my Borsalino hat and decided it was best just to take my galleys like a man.

"Hey, fellas," I said, giving Jimmy and Leo my best well-meaning-private-eye-in-a-jam smiles. "I didn't know the zoo gave out furloughs."

They swarmed all over me—no rough stuff yet, but showing me they would know how to go about it.

Jimmy's voice was as big as he was. "Mr. Santucci wants his money, Elston. A grand."

"Where am I supposed to come up with a thousand dollars?"

"You're a private eye," Leadpipe said, his voice rising like Lazarus from the dark. "Go private eyeing."

"It ain't that easy, apeface."

Leadpipe's face got as red as the ketchup stain on his shirt. "How much you got, Elston?"

I was about $999 short of a grand, and when I told the Sumo twins that, they proceeded to beat half of it out of me until I was lying there on the hot pavement of the parking lot bleeding all over myself.

Jimmy laughed like Dracula and said:

"Next week you better have all of it, or else—"

He moved his sausage finger slowly across his throat and cold chills did the Jitterbug down my spine. The last time I checked, moving your finger across your throat wasn't a sign they wanted to buy me a beer, it was meant that if I didn't come up with Bedbug's money, someone was going to find me floating ass-up in the Gulf of Santa Rita.

♣♣♣

After my ten rounds with Leo and Jimmy I kicked the Electra's engine over, crawled through the gears, and drove over to my favorite watering hole.

The Red Carpet was down on Canal Street, a block away from my apartment, in the lonely warehouse district along the waterfront. You had to go down a couple of steps to reach the entrance and before you reached it you could smell what you were walking into.

There wasn't much light, just a few dim bulbs in the ceiling and a neon Burgie Beer sign sputtering on the wall. It was a place of burnished wood and chased mirrors, an Irish flag hanging behind the barback and faded photographs of long-deceased prizefighters. There were only three people at the bar. A middle-aged bim painted up like an Iroquois and two old-timers with Johnnie Walker noses slopping down their sugar ration stamps. The Red Carpet wasn't a dive; it was a dump, but it was good enough for what I needed.

Angie was working behind the bar, and that's what I needed. She was a looker of mythic proportions—eyes like a piercing cry, a lion's-mane of dirty blonde hair, and a full red mouth that would have sent Shakespeare thumbing through a thesaurus.

A wealth of woman whose emotions could be hard or soft or frightening as hell; men were Angie's speed, and she liked to go the limit, but don't get the idea she was easy. I've seen her give a few goons the brush off the hard way. When it came to quick action she could whip off a shoe and crack a skull before you could bat an eye.

"Hey, sweetheart," I called out. "That's an uneasy smile."

"You want smiles," Angie said, mopping the bar top down with a dirty rag. "I'm beat out to the bone. Slopping giggle juice to drunks and sailors all day. I should have stayed in school and been a veterinarian."

"Yeah, but you hate animals."

"I hate drunks, too. What's your point, Elston?"

Angie started pouring me an Old Scratch Amber without me asking for it. Yeah, she knew what I liked in more ways than one.

I dropped my goose on a wobbly stool at the end of the bar and wrapped my feet around the chromium rungs.

"How does my tab stand these days, Ang?"

"Like a three-legged dog," she said. "Worried about it?"

She was wearing blue and black plaid clam digger pants and a white Hardy O shirt. I leaned over the bar and disrobed her optically.

She put the beer in front of my face, fired up two cigarettes and handed me one. I tasted her lipstick on it and suddenly my heart was pounding in my ears so loud I could barely hear anything else.

"What happened to your face this time, Elston," Angie was saying.

When my eyes first caught on the pale figure in the mirror behind the bar, I was startled because I thought it was someone else. Thanks to Leo and Jimmy my face was a gruesome Halloween mask, hastily painted in every shade of black and blue.

"I ran into a screen door," I told Angie, running a hand over my meaty face.

"Must have been one mean screen door," she said, pouring me a whiskey chaser to go along with my beer. "Here, you look like you could use this."

I polished off the chaser in one swallow, hoping the guys that had used it before me didn't have anything contagious.

"How's the private eye business?" Angie asked.

"Scarce as hen's teeth. It's so bad I can't even afford to buy my own drinks."

She made a face like a little girl, pursing her lips until the dimples showed in her cheeks. "It's on the house."

"Thanks."

She poured me another beer and ran her eyes over my face again. "Ah, Elston, every time you get beat up I ache all over."

"*You* ache all over?"

I got the dimples again. "Yes, I have a very compassionate psyche."

"Want to come over to my place tonight?"

"Not tonight."

"What happened to that compassionate psyche?"

"It's not *that* compassionate. Besides, I have a date tonight."

I hunched forward and made love to my beer. The way things were going that was the only thing I'd be making love to tonight.

"Who's your date with this time?" I asked, in a voice that could have split firewood. "The doctor from Santa Barbara or the lawyer from Mission Viejo?"

There was a time when she would have gotten red and slammed me across the jaw. There was a time when she would have broken off a date with Rudolph Valentino to put away a cheeseburger in a diner with me. Those times have flown.

"Don't be cruel, Elston," she said, without much cheer. "How come you're always getting beat up anyway?"

"I owe someone money and when I can't pay, he likes to take a pound out of my flesh for collateral."

"Maybe I could help."

"Got a thousand dollars?"

Her eyes darkened. "I don't have that kind of money. I wish I did, but I don't. Maybe I could get you a loan in the bank?"

"Thanks, I'd love to be alone with you in the bank, but I need the money fast."

"You need to stop betting away all your money on the bangtails down at the track."

"Watch it," I said. "I'm not above slapping a dame around if she deserves it. I've slapped dames before. All right, maybe spanked is a better word."

I faked a right hook at her and she fake ducked. I looked at my watch. It was time to go. Angie had a date with a doctor or a lawyer or an Indian chief and I had a date with my empty apartment and a bottle of Old Crow.

I grabbed my hat off the bar and started for the door. I was almost out when I heard Angie say:

"Take care of yourself, Elston."

There was real concern in her voice and I turned around to look at her. She reminded me in some ways of my first wife, but in some ways she didn't.

"What are you going to do about your money problems, Elston?"

"I don't know. Maybe I'll sell my blood to the Red Cross."

Very slowly a smile worked itself on Angie's face. "Bela Lugosi couldn't get a grand's worth of blood out of that body of yours."

"Now, now, kitty cat, don't scratch."

I put my hat on carefully, blew her a kiss across the bar and waded out the door.

The streetlights had kicked in and the working crowd had cleared out an hour ago and the city was going through its metamorphous as the night closed in around it.

I got in my car and drove home.

I lived at the intersection of A Street and Water Street back then, right behind the *St. Pauli Girl* billboard, which was something of a local landmark. She looked like the blonde virgin/whore who used to babysit your little sister when you were a kid. Her job was to make you fall in love with her and drink more St. Pauli Girl beer. From the front she was an incredibly well-endowed girl, but from my apartment all you could see were the iron gurters and struts holding her up. When I got there I parked in a spot in the alley behind a green garbage bin. There was always the chance that the police might mistake my heap for an abandoned vehicle and haul it away, but that night, I risked it.

Chapter Two

It was another stale and windless weekend, the kind that makes people do sweaty, secret things. I was sweating it out in my office on the corner of Ivar and Highland Avenues, trying to figure out how I was going to pay-off Bedbug, when *she* came in.

Her dress was made out of something shiny like satin. Hellfire red. The most tempting color since Eve winked at Adam.

"I'm looking for a Mr. Elston Brand," she said, rubbing her hand up and down her forearm absently.

She had full red lips designed to be nibbled on and curly black hair that fell in ringlets like ravens dancing over her shoulder; a darker version of Venus-on-A-Half-Shell.

"I'm Elston Brand," I told her.

She was very prim and proper, like the doll of a rich girl, very delicate and not often played with. "Elston Brand? The private detective?"

"That's what it says on the door."

She thought for a moment, her forehead creasing. "Actually, it says Al's Sewer and Drain Cleaning."

"The card must have fallen off," I mumbled. "Come in."

She came in and I got a good glimpse of her eyes for the first time. They were dark green and as mesmerizing as the flames in a fire, but something about those eyes told me that they were carrying a lot of memories.

She drew herself up importantly. "My name is Melissa Barrett."

The name meant nothing to me, but she seemed to think it should.

With a flick of my wrist I showed her the customer's chair. She sat down, crossed her legs and smoothed her dress over her knees with a caressing motion. It didn't need smoothing.

I snagged my swivel-squeaker with my toe, pulled it up behind my desk and sat down. "Okay, Mrs. Barrett, let's get down to business. Why did you come see me?"

She was all fragrance, bad nerves, and shy smiles. "You're a man for hire. I want to hire you."

I got a Lucky Strike out and rolled it around my fingers. "Why do you want to hire me?"

"Because I'm going to be murdered," she said, her voice like a whip on a horse's back.

"Who's going to murder you, Mrs. Barrett?"

"My husband," she said, sending that horse round and round the track.

The big M word. The gravy train for private dicks like me.

"Why does your husband want to kill you?"

Her eyes tightened. "For the insurance."

I took the cigarette out of my mouth and looked at it aimlessly and stuck it back in. "How much is the policy worth?"

"Three hundred thousand dollars. Triple indemnity."

I laughed, but it was a short laugh. *Three hundred grand?* I started wondering if this bird was crazy.

"What does your husband do, Mrs. Barrett?"

"He's the Alderman of Los Angeles County."

My mind put two and two together and got a five-figure number.

"Barrett? *Robert* Barrett? He's your husband?"

Her head bobbled up and down like an egg boiling in water.

I didn't have to ask who Alderman Robert Barrett was. His picture was in the Santa Rita Times at least twice a week, kissing babies or shaking hands with some political hotshot or another. Some people in the know were saying he was in line to become the next governor of California.

"Robert Barrett is your husband?" I said again, trying to sink my teeth into it.

She closed her eyes, and after a few rhythmical movements, the answer came under her breath.

"How long have you been married?" I asked her.

There was a strange lilting to her voice when she said, "Almost two years now. Robert and I were married two years ago this September. That's when he took out the policy. We both took out policies."

"Other than the insurance money, what makes you think he wants to kill you?"

Some flicker of almost unbearable emotion came and went in her eyes. "He's having an affair, Mr. Brand."

"Why don't you just get a divorce?"

"My husband has many ambitions. Ambitions that tend to put him in the public eye. The scandal of an affair and divorce would ruin him. But if I had an accident—"

"Do you have any proof?"

"That's where you come in."

"You want me to follow your husband around for a few days, maybe snap some photographs of him and this other woman?"

"Yes. I had a locksmith duplicate the key to Robert's office. You could poke around a bit after he leaves." She looked around my shabby office with an idle but raking glance. "Come now, Mr. Brand. We both know that times are tough with the war going on. A man in your profession could always use the money."

The way she said it was just enough to make me look up at her and frown. "What makes you think that?"

Her feet were in a diminutive pair of metallic-suede pumps, pert, saucy, without backs, without sides, without toes, in fact with scarcely anything but dagger-like heels and a couple of straps. The toes of her right foot kept waving hypnotically at me.

Her tone was light and calculating. "This is Santa Rita, Mr. Brand, not Los Angeles. In a town like Santa Rita, there can't be a huge demand for your type of services."

She was right, but I didn't want her to know that. "I get plenty of work, Mrs. Barrett," I said, with more nonchalance than I felt. "So much in fact that I can afford to kick your pretty little gluteus out of here and never think twice about it."

I was acting tough, but she saw through me like an old piece of tattered cheesecloth, and I swear I even saw her wink.

"What brought you to Santa Rita anyway, Mr. Brand?" she asked. "I can tell by your accent that you weren't born here."

She was right again. Right on the damn money. I was born and raised in the Midwest, in Battle Creek, Michigan. After high school I enlisted in the Navy, served four years in the Philippines, went back home, got married, became a beat cop on the North Side until a misunderstanding concerning the police chief's daughter, a jar of Bramwell's honey and a gorilla mask ended my promising career and my marriage. The next thing I knew I'd booked a red-eye flight to Anywhere. And Anywhere just happened to be Santa Rita.

But I wasn't about to tell Melissa Barrett any of that.

"Where I'm from and where I've been doesn't matter," I told her. "It's what I've done with where I've been that should be of interest to you, Mrs. Barrett."

The dim lighting of the office made a soft halo around her coldly beautiful face. We sat there staring at each other for a full half minute. I was trying to stare her down but it couldn't be done. I felt myself licking my lips instead.

After a while, she said, "By the way, how did you get those cuts and bruises on your face?"

"Occupational hazards," I said. "Comes with the territory."

She let her lips remain parted when she said, "So do you want the job, Mr. Brand?"

"I'm expensive."

"I can afford you."

LACE & WHISKEY

I was considering my options. There weren't many. I needed all the money I could scrape together and the last time I checked, my checking account could kiss the sidewalk without stooping. Matrimonial and divorce work were my meat and potatoes, but I'd been practically living on noodles and rice. Sure, once in a blue moon I was thrown a security detail from one of the big movie studios, asked to babysit one of the new spoiled starlets with names like Vivien, Hedy, or Lana, but those jobs were becoming fewer and farther between, what with the War Production Board cutting back on allotments to all the major movie studios.

The way I figured it, I could take the case, dig around in Alderman Barrett's life for a few days and collect a nice fat paycheck to boot. After all that's the kind of work a private dick like me does—hot, thankless, sleazy work. I spend most of my time following husbands who are following their neighbor's wives, playing tag with non-support deadbeats or hiding in closets watching yucky people do yucky things. Most people want their lives to be predictable. You go to work, battle traffic at the end of the day, kiss the kiddies, have a cocktail, make love to the wife once or twice a week, no surprises. You put in your years selling your soul down at the factory, retire, collect your pension, and then die. But I ain't like that. For fifty bucks a week and reasonable expenses, I stick my nose where no one else will and usually get my brains beat in for the effort. Why? Because I need the sleaze and uncertainty of the city, a world one shade blacker than black, where justice can be bought for the price of a beer and where depravity lies around every corner. I need the Dewar's and the dames and the double-crosses. That's the tune I danced to, brother.

"I get a hundred a week," I told Melissa Barrett, shooting high. "Plus expenses."

The smile settled in one corner of her mouth. "Very well then, we've got a deal."

She held out her hand and I shook it, a brief touch that sent my skin crawling up my spine. I couldn't tell if I was shaking hands with Mati Hari or Mother Mary.

She stood up, smoothed down her dress again and edged toward the door. I moved my legs to give her a little room to pass, but she still let her hip brush against me, and I got as weak as if I had just climbed out of a hot Turkish bath. I couldn't tell if she did it on purpose, but I like to think she did.

"Robert typically leaves his office around five o'clock."

She held out the key and I picked it out of her fingers.

"One more thing, Mrs. Barrett," I called out to her as she was drifting toward the door.

She turned around and stared at me. "Yes?"

"Why me?" I asked.

"I don't understand the question, Mr. Brand?"

"Why hire me of all people? A private eye you found in the phone directory?"

"You were recommended to me by a friend who said—"

I held up my hand like a traffic cop. "Save it, sister. No friend of yours is going to recommend *me*."

She looked gorgeous and sharp. She looked gorgeous because she couldn't help it and she looked sharp because she was.

"Okay, you caught me, Mr. Brand. I have to confess. I picked your name at random out of the phone directory."

Now we were getting somewhere. Where I didn't quite know yet.

There was a far-away look on her face. Genuine? Who knows what genuine is anymore?

"I didn't know what I'd find when I came here," she began, her eyes narrow and as hard as jet. "But you remind me of someone I once knew a long time ago. Someone I was very close with. Someone I could always trust."

It was a nice speech, but I had other things on my mind. Little green things with pictures of dead presidents on them.

"I'll take the first hundred in advance," I told her.

She calmly reached into her purse and took out several loose bills. "There's five hundred dollars there, Mr. Brand. That should cover you for a while."

I took the money and held it in my hands. It felt like I was holding a small fuzzy elephant.

"I'll call you in a few days," I told her.

She took out a matchbook from the Palomino Club and scribbled down her number.

"Where do you live?" I asked. "Just in case something happens."

"What could happen?"

"In my business anything can happen."

Her eyes were steady, unblinking. "We have a house up on Telegraph Road."

"Nice neighborhood."

"Yes, Mr. Brand. It is."

And with that, she turned and walked toward the door.

She had a nice walk, like a ballerina, not slumped down on her shoulders, but held up in the small of her back, with just as much wiggle as a woman could get away with nowadays.

Her shadow was the last part of her to go. It trailed slowly after her, upright against the wall, its head down a little. It stayed on a moment, after she herself was already gone. Then it slipped off the wall after her, and it was gone too.

Nothing was left there but the door and the smell of her good perfume, lingering like a dying candle. It wasn't any of that cheap stuff some broads try to pass off as classy these days. This was the good stuff. Some real snazzy toilet water.

I went over to the window, spread the slats of the blinds and watched her on the street as she got into a sharp little Aston Martin. Red. Like a pepper. A nice little toy to catch any man's eye. When she bent down to get in, her dress went up a couple of inches and my eyes were momentarily unhinged by the sight of her stockined legs. They were two of the nicest getaway sticks I'd ever seen.

She drove off and I went over to my desk and counted the money. Five hundred. On the nose.

I started thinking about the things I could do with it.

Then I started thinking about Melissa Barrett.

Then I started thinking about the things I could do with Melissa Barrett.

I got out the phone book and looked up Robert Barrett. He had his office on the first floor of the Dainbridge Criminal Justice Center on West Temple. I copied down the address and stuck it in my pocket. Then I got my leather shoulder harness out of my desk, strapped it on, and slipped my .38 Smith & Wesson with the Mershon Sure Grip handle into it. I loved that gun like the brother I never had. It'd seen me through plenty of scrapes in the past.

I strapped the lower strap, looped it around both shoulders, grabbed my Kodak Six-20, and went down to the street.

The heat was on, sending everyone indoors and clasping the city in a wet and soppy embrace. I didn't mind the heat. With everyone else scurrying to the movie houses and department stores for the artificial assuage of air conditioning, I had the city to myself.

I got in my Electra and drove over to West Temple. When I got there I parked my heap diagonally across the street from the Dainbridge Building, a large pile of gray stone which was as close as the city came to a skyscraper.

I sat back against the cushions and waited for something to happen. Just what, I couldn't say.

Nothing happened.

I had a big flask of Four Roses whiskey with me. I used it often enough to keep me interested.

I smoked a lot of cigarettes and snapped a few photos of random people doing random things. I listened to Roy Hughes and the Los Angeles Angels beat the San Francisco Seals 3-2 on the car radio. I watched a bob-tailed lizard stop and cock his head at me, then make a desperate dash across the street only to be squashed by a Red and White taxi.

Late in the afternoon it started to rain, splashing knee-high off the sidewalks and filling the gutters. It drummed on the hood of the Electra and beat down on the taut material of the top, leaking in at places and making a pool on the floorboards for me to put my feet in.

At five-thirty Robert Barrett came out of the Dainbridge Building and got in a shiny new

Lincoln Continental. He was a good-looking guy, tall and dark with a lot of wavy gray hair brushed back from his forehead. He looked a little like Tyrone Power. I thought Melissa had told me he was fat and old and bald. On the other hand, maybe I imagined that. Maybe I wanted him to be fat and old and bald; but Robert Barrett, Alderman-God of the San Fernando Valley, was not fat and old and bald. Like I said, he was tall and had a lot of hair. Women like guys that are tall and have a lot of hair. I could tell he was one of those guys that women liked, and therefore, I hated him immediately.

Barrett drove west on Lenox Avenue. I drove west on Lenox Avenue. At Echo Park he turned south and I tailed him easily from a block back. I followed him up through the winding roads of the Hollywood Hills. He took a turn and another turn, and then we got on the entrance to the new freeway.

The stream of traffic was fairly heavy; homeward-bound executives making speed to get home to cocktails and the Bob Hope Show on the radio, but as we passed the city limits the traffic thinned to a meager dribble. I was going to have to hang back as far as I could or Barrett would glom on to me, so I let his Lincoln pull away until the ruby-red taillights were merely dots in the distance.

At the end of the freeway, the road swung to the left, with nothing on the right hand side but a hill and the HOLLYWOODLAND sign and an occasional drop of 2,200 feet.

Telegraph Road was nestled on top of a bluff smiling down on the twinkling panorama of lights of the city below. Barrett turned right on Telegraph. It had no sidewalks. Nobody walked in this neighborhood, not even the mailman.

The million dollar shacks lining the boulevard were set well back with rolling green lawns that smelled like money. Some had high walls of brick, some had low walls, some had ornamental iron fences, all designed to keep the riff-and-raff like me out.

Barrett pulled the Lincoln into a driveway, opened the hydraulic gate, and drove up to a garage that might have held a dozen Lincoln's if you squeezed them all in with a shoehorn.

I turned the Electra around, parked under the shadows of a tamarind tree and killed the engine. Then I went into a private consultation with my flask of Four Roses and sat there watching the place. It must have gone to twenty rooms at least and nothing left out. Only a moat and turret short of a castle. The showplace home of Santa Rita, the one you took out-of-town relatives to see; a big solid cool-looking Colonial with a terra-cotta tile roof and leaded front windows downstairs and up. An acre or so of grass sloping down to a big swimming pool the color of a marlin beside the backyard.

Dusk came early, then it deepened to dark. A solid, slow-moving hour crawled by. No cars came up or down the hill. The street was deserted. I couldn't see inside the house, but I knew Melissa Barrett was in there somewhere. Then a single flash of hard electric light leaked out of an upstairs bedroom and a woman's shadow passed it.

I could almost picture her. The warm, inviting body and the long blue-black hair. The little cupid's nose and the large pouty lips. I thought I was going to go batty thinking of her, and when I couldn't take it any longer, I fired up the Electra and pointed it back down the hill toward Santa Rita, to my little one-bedroom dump on Water

Street, a dank grotto in the very bowels of the Old City.

My room was on the second floor of a two-story brick monstrosity rife with hucksters, hustlers, hookers and hoods, above a nefarious chop-suey place that occupied the entire ground floor. By the time I got there I was feeling pretty rotten about it. I wanted a place like the Barrett's. A place with a driveway and a garage. A place with more than one bedroom and plumbing that actually worked on a regular basis. Instead, I was stuck with a cold-water pad that smelled like misery and Kung Pao Chicken.

I parked in the alley, climbed the rickety back staircase, went in and ate a leftover pork chop, moldy applesauce, some cold rice, and washed it all down with a warm bottle of Tecate Beer. I lighted a cigarette, flipped the match in the ashtray where it turned into a charred arc, and wondered how the hell I'd ever wound up here with the rest of the losers, wannabes, wayward starlets, and any other form of doomed suckfish you could think of.

I sat at the kitchen table and glowered around the room, at the cheap plastic window blinds, the shabby mission furniture, the threadbare carpet and dingy walls. That sinister Oriental den downstairs had a lurid red neon sign that shimmered tigerishly in at me.

I opened another beer, set fire to another gasper and sat around the kitchen table smoking and feeling sorry for myself. I had nothing better to do and no place better to go and right then I didn't like myself very much. And I couldn't stop thinking about something lovely, something with green eyes and raven's hair and a body that looked warm, inviting.

Chapter Three

The next day I went back to Barrett's office; and the next, and the next. Every day it was the same thing. He'd arrive at eight in the morning, go out for a few hours at noon, come back, and leave for the day at five or five-thirty. Just your average everyday workaholic; immersed in a system of work, produce, consume, work, produce, consume.

Then on the third day, right around noon, a bird with curves like the Indy 500 walked into his office. She'd be hard to miss with curves like that. She looked like she belonged in New York or Paris or Milan.

She was blonde as hell, wearing a lot of black, with a Ziegfeld body and long skinny legs sticking out of black high-heeled pumps sharp enough to pierce a man's heart. I propped my Kodak Six-20 on the dash of the Electra and aimed it at her. She went into Barrett's office and a few minutes later the two of them came out together, all smiles and touchy-touchy.

They got in Barrett's Lincoln and I tailed them over to the Drake Hotel. Real swanky place, surrounded by palms and jacarandas. A period showpiece, painted pale ochre, fourteen floors high and decorated at the top with bas-reliefs and stone gargoyles.

I waited in my car for a few minutes after they went in, then I crossed the street and entered the shiny bowels of the Drake. The guy holding down the reception desk was an overdressed Latino who looked like a cockroach ready to slip under the floorboards. He stood there hating everything and everybody. I passed him a Lincoln and asked what room Barrett was in.

He looked at me like I was loco.

I dug out another Lincoln.

The bill left my fingers magically.

"1120," the Latino said with the kind of smile you get from people who have a hard time smiling.

I walked up one flight of marble steps to a mezzanine and pushed the button for the elevator. When it came I got in and told the attendant I wanted to go up to the eleventh floor. He stared at my shabby suit and I stared back at him until he reluctantly took me up.

The long hallway was bright clean and as silent as a winter night. I walked past room 1120. Then I walked past it a second time, stopping at the gray olivewood door.

I put my ear up to the panel and I could hear them going at it like a pair of wild dogs. Hell, it even made *me* blush.

The door across the hall suddenly opened and a rich old bag wearing the hide of some dead animal stood there looking at me like I was some kind of pervert.

"Surveillance," I whispered.

She rolled her eyes, twisted the dead animal around her neck, gave me a "humph," and went away.

I put my ear back to the door. Robert Barrett and his afternoon caller were still going at it.

I stood there thinking.

So, I thought, Robert Barrett had a motive to kill his wife. The oldest motive in the books. He was screwing the socks off another woman, and with his wife out of the way, he could collect the three-hundred grand on the insurance policy and fly off to Borra Borra or wherever people like Robert Barrett flew off to.

Yeah, I knew it was thin. About as thin as my ex-wife's cooking, but I couldn't wait to tell Melissa. I don't know what I expected. Maybe she'd be so distraught she'd fall into my arms like you see in an Ingrid Bergman movie.

Something like that.

I got in my beat-up Buick and drove back to my office. When I got there, I went in and fished out Melissa's number and got on the blower.

The operator rang the number and Melissa answered on the third ring.

"Mrs. Barrett," I said. "I've got some bad news. I don't think you're going to like it."

"What is it?" she asked.

"Not over the phone," I said.

"Why?" she said sarcastically. "Is your line bugged?"

"Usually," I said seriously. "Can we meet somewhere?"

"Where?"

We agreed to meet at a place I knew of called *Le Petite Shrimp House* at 435 E. 43rd Street. It had been just another second-rate dive until recently a reporter from the Santa Rita Times wandered in and mentioned it in his column as a good place to relax after work if you liked peace and quiet. The next day it became a first-rate pub with the after-office crowd and now it was anything but peace and quiet.

I knew the bouncer—or the *doorman* as he was now called—and it was still early enough to get a table without having to pass a Lincoln between handshakes. He gave me a table in the back, which was fine by me.

It was Thursday, five p.m., Happy Hour.

The air inside was thick with perfume and cigarette smoke and the dry smell of expensive martinis and lots of people; swarms of skirts and suits uniformly released from their nine-to-five prisons and out on the prowl.

A few minutes into my first whiskey Melissa came in. She was wearing yellow now; a summer dress that contrasted weirdly and exotically with her dark hair and creamy complexion. She was bare-legged, with yellow open-toe sandals to match the dress.

I waved her down and she walked over with all the unhurried smoothness of poured honey. Half the bar—both men *and* women—turned to look at her. She was one of those dames that demanded attention; someone who could pull off looking like a million bucks wearing a paper napkin.

"What'll have to drink?" I asked her.

"What are you having?"

"Whiskey."

"That'll do."

I looked across the table at her. There was something about her eyes, and the fish-spine delicacy of her face. She had those eyes, you know the ones, those droopy little eyes that can make a man just about do anything, murder and the trading of your soul not exempt.

She drank her whiskey very slowly. I drank mine very fast. I took out my deck of Luckies, lit one, and let the smoke trickle out through my nostrils.

There was a long silence.

Finally, Melissa said, "What is it that you needed so urgently to tell me?"

I didn't know how to tell her, so I just told her. I recited the whole incident, about the Drake and her husband's afternoon rendezvous, and let her digest it.

When I finished she didn't say anything. She just kept looking down at her wedding ring, a gold band with a football-shaped diamond sitting on top of it. Her face was tight, the tip of her tongue darting out occasionally over her lower lip.

"Who is she?" she said after a while.

"I don't know yet."

"Do you have proof?"

"I snapped some photographs of them going into the Drake."

"It could have been a business associate."

"It wasn't a business associate. Unless one of your husband's business associates has a habit of howling like a coyote."

I paused and waited to see what she'd say next.

She didn't say anything, so I said, "Why'd you do it?"

Her face hardened. "Why did I do what?"

"Marry him."

In a voice that had the crisp clarity of static electricity, she said, "You want to hear all the desperate details, Mr. Brand? Fine. Robert's first priority has always been his career, and my best guess is he's been seeing other women since before we were engaged, but it's not as if I didn't know what I was getting into."

"Do you love him?"

"I love his money. His money pleases me, maybe because I spent my whole life without any of it. Maybe that makes me a bad person, I don't know. I'm used to the money now. A person gets used to having things, Mr. Brand. I'm his wife. He bought me and I make him pay heavily for me. The best food, the best cars, the best clothes. So now he owns me."

"Why don't you leave him?"

"I live in a maze, Mr. Brand. A strange, blind maze, and all the little twisting paths lead back to Robert. I can't leave him. He'd kill me if I ever tried. He has friends. A lot of powerful friends."

I sucked on my grit. "He's the Alderman not the President. If you really think he's capable of murder, then maybe this is a job better suited for the boys in blue."

Her voice was a dry rustle of sound. "Robert owns the police. The law is where you buy it in this town."

She had a good point. I'd seen enough corruption in this town to make Al Capone cringe like a schoolgirl.

I smashed out my cigarette and lit another one. Melissa wanted one too this time. Her long, slim fingers handled the cigarette like a pro and I lit it for her across the table.

After it was lit, she stayed leaning toward me for a brief moment, looking at me from her half-lowered eyes while the smoke drifted between us. I stared at her, thinking to myself what a nice round face she had, and other nice round parts, too. I wanted to reach over the table and throw her on the floor and make love to her right there in front of everyone. It was pure, unadulterated, animal magnetism.

I knew there must have been a quiver in my voice when I said, "I guess I could poke around your husband's office some night after he leaves. See if I can find anything more discriminating. But if I do find something, sooner or later we're going to have to go to the police."

"Robert is leaving early tomorrow night," she said, her sea-green eyes square and steady on mine. "He's flying to Sacramento. He'll be away for a few days and no one else will be around. If you did this one last thing for me, I'll make sure you're well compensated."

Maybe it was the opulent sound of her voice. Maybe it was the deep liquid eyes that got deeper as she stared into mine. But at that moment I think I would have done anything she asked.

We finished our drinks and I walked her out of the place, enjoying the envious looks I got along the way.

Outside I took her to the valet stand where a blonde kid who looked like he should be a lifeguard flagged down her Aston. After he got the car, the blonde kid held his hand out. He didn't want me to shake it. I struggled in my pants pocket and managed a quarter with lint on it. He didn't seem too happy when I handed it to him.

I told Melissa goodnight and watched her crawl into the shiny little car. She moved very slowly, as if she were climbing into a bleak future, and I couldn't tell whose future was bleaker, hers or mine.

Chapter Four

That night I legged it over to police headquarters. I had a friend in Vice named Frank Merriwell. When I got there he was sitting behind an old metal desk that looked like it came from army surplus. His office was bland and institutional, like the rest of the building, furnished with that peculiar sordid hideousness only municipalities can achieve.

Frank was playing a game of solitaire, the cards spread out in front of him, and he was looking for a black queen to put on his king of diamonds.

"Ever catch yourself cheating at that game?" I asked.

He looked up, registered little if any shock at seeing me. "It's no fun if you cheat."

"And very little fun if you don't."

Frank was a long, tall gallows of a man, with steely gray eyes and yellow skin, a shopworn cop one cigarette away from emphysema. He was the first cop I met when I came to Santa Rita ten years ago. We used to drink out of the same bottle back then, but not that much lately.

I gave him the rag end of a smile. "How come you never tip a few with me anymore, Frank?"

He leaned back until the chair squeaked. His face looked like a map of Los Angeles, full of the disgust of the streets and the thickening effects off too much booze and too many cigarettes. "I'm married with three teenage kids. I got no time anymore to tip a few with a private star like you, Elston. Nowadays I do my drinking on my own."

"Wife's got you on a pretty short leash, huh, Frank?"

He looked gimlet-eyed at me. "Yep, pretty short."

I made a beeline for the coffee pot. It had something in it that looked like the stuff the dinosaurs got trapped in up at La Brea. I poured myself some anyway and burnt my tongue on it.

"Jesus, Frank, what did you cut this coffee with, a torch?"

"Get your own damn coffee if you don't like it."

He took out a pack of Pall Mall's with some miles on it and lighted a cigarette. I borrowed his lighter and set fire to my own gasper.

"What do you want, Elston?" Frank said, his Pall Mall bobbing in his mouth like a fishing lure.

"Who says I want anything, Frank?"

"Elston Brand always wants something."

I felt the grin twist the corner of my mouth. "Just some information, that's all."

Like every cop from the beginning of time, I knew Frank coveted doughnuts the way an amorous dog covets an ankle, so before I went up there I'd stopped at a *Yum Yum's* across the street and got a dozen jellies. I pulled the bag out from behind my back and Frank glanced up excitedly, like a kid on Christmas morn.

"What do you have in the bag, Elston?"

I gave him the bag. He practically ripped my hand off grabbing it, peeked inside, and shoved a jelly in his beak. He finished it in two bites and shoved in another.

"What's so special about the jellies?" I asked him.

He shrugged. "The jelly."

I had another pull at the coffee. "What do you know about a guy named Robert Barrett?" I asked with all the subtlety of a shotgun. After all, Frank had ten more jellies and a solitaire game to get back to.

He leaned forward on his desk, the expression on his face as if his shorts were too tight. "Do you mean Alderman Barrett?"

"Yeah, that's right."

His eyes got big and he started sweating like a dog in a Chinese restaurant. "Stay away from him, Elston. Barrett is way out of your league. He's out of everyone's league. Goes around looking at everyone like they were ants and he was a big shoe. You know how it is. You want to swing a deal with the state, and the first thing you know you find Alderman Barrett in your path. And you either work with him or you don't swing a deal."

"That big, huh?"

Frank stuffed his face with another jelly. "Yeah, that big. He's the top pillow in this town, Elston."

"Is there any dirt on him?" I asked. "Everyone's got a little dirt on them."

Frank's expression was sour. "Barrett is associated with the trouble boys, if you know what I mean. His protection has got protection. Guys with big guns; hatchet men that'll let some air into your skull just for the fun of it. Guys that'll kick out your teeth and then shoot you for mumbling. But just try to prove it. He's untouchable. Clean as a Beverly Hills whore. There was a case he was involved in about a year ago, a small-time hood named Joey Chill accused Barrett of extorting several hundred grand's worth of heroin from his operation, but the whole thing was buried faster than a pack of dogs on a three-legged cat."

"How come?"

"No proof. It was all hush-hush. It was never leaked to the papers and the heroin was never found."

"What happened to Joey Chill?"

Frank shrugged. "What happens to all the small-time hoods sooner or later? Last February his body was found in a dumpster. Someone had given him a second neck. Opened him up like a Thanksgiving turkey."

"Was Barrett ever tied to the murder?"

"Are you kidding me? He's the Alderman of Los Angeles County for Christ sakes. He packs a lot of currency in his pants." Frank looked at me suspiciously. "Why you sniffing around Barrett's drainpipe anyway?"

I shrugged. "Confidential, Frank."

He finished his third jelly and lit another cigarette. "You're a nice egg, Elston, but you've got yourself poured into the wrong pan this time, my friend. My advice to you is to leave Barrett alone."

Chapter Five

After midnight I drove to Barrett's office and parked in the shadows on the other side of the street. There was a mutter of thunder in the distance. A slice of the horizon lightened for a moment, and then it started to rain, beating against my windshield, thick drops flattening out and washing down the glass in tiny waves. Washing away the sins of the city.

I took out the key Melissa had given me, twirled it around in my fingers, then got out and crossed the street, looking up once at the sky overhead. It was a slow, fat rain that took a while to collect on my hat brim before it cascaded down in front of my eyes.

I took my lighter out and spun the little wheel. There was a spark, then a blue flame that sputtered in the rain. I touched it to the end of a damp cigarette and watched it smolder and flame up. There was a wild crackle in the air. The wind hummed in the electric wires. The night was all weird and quiet and loud with the wind and rain at the same time.

I went around to the alley where the rain was falling past the arc lights like a long silver sword. I kept to the edges, one hand tracing building, feeling my way along the damp wall as I spiraled down into the gloom.

A mangy yellow tomcat with a torn ear whined in the night and I almost jumped out of my socks. It was licking its chops and working on a bird it had just killed, its yellow eyes glowing up at me.

I ankled past her, noticed that the bird was all gone except for a few wing feathers, and found the side door to Barrett's office.

I stuck the key in and turned the lock. The door opened silently on good springs.

I stepped inside and flicked my pocket power light and lit my way among the plush office furniture and indoor palms.

In the middle of the room was a receptionist's desk with a nameplate that read "THERESA KRAMER" and an office in back with Barrett's name stenciled on the frosted door.

I went around the reception desk and into Barrett's office. On the far side of the room was the usual broad executive desk with the usual high-backed padded leather chair. On the wall behind the desk was a large oil painting of a coquettish nymph lying in a field. That was kind of nice.

I shined my flash on the desk and walked over. There was a sleek onyx pen and pencil set on top of it. There were no photographs of Melissa on the desk. That was odd, I thought. Most guys have pictures of their wife on their desk, especially if they were even half as beautiful as Melissa was, but Robert Barrett didn't have one single picture.

The wastebasket was full of crumpled-up paper. I almost wasted ten minutes going through it rather carefully. I sat in Barrett's leather chair and pawed through the drawers of the desk. There was nothing in them but an assortment of legal papers, affidavit's or court orders or something; I couldn't make out. I slammed the drawers shut and started taking the place apart.

I didn't find a damn thing.

I leaned back in the chair and looked around the plushy silence of the room. There had to be something I was missing. A secret compartment in the desk or a hidden safe somewhere. Guys like Barrett always had them.

I spun around in the chair and my eyes fell on the coquettish nymph. I rubbed my chin and stood up and pulled one edge of the frame.

And there it was. A square black metal wall safe with a Chicago brand double-sided lock. Nothing I hadn't seen before.

I took out my disk tumbler pick and jimmied the spring on the lock. A few seconds later I popped the safe open without too much effort and found myself staring back at a big, ugly .38 automatic.

Next to the .38 was a manila envelope with a rubber band around it. Under the envelope was a black attaché case.

I took out the envelope and slid the rubber band off. Inside were photographs. Black and white eight-by-ten glossies of Barrett's lunch-time caller. The bird with curves like the Indy 500.

She was naked and doing a variety of tricks. I didn't think a person could be that flexible. She was like the Rubber Lady in the circus.

I kept one of the photographs for myself and put the rest back in the envelope. Then I took out the attaché case and put it on top of the desk. It was locked, hinged at the back. I used my pick and went right through those hinges.

The case popped open with a loud snap.

In it were bindles of cash and a dozen or so plastic bags filled with white powder. I took out one of the bags and sliced it with the file. Then I dipped my pinky into the powder and licked it. My head took off for Mars. I felt the way I had when I'd first taken a lower lip full of snuff as a kid back home in Battle Creek.

I licked my pinky again and stuck it back in the bag. Then I licked it a third time. There were little fireworks going off in my brain now.

Heroin.

The cash in the attaché case was stacked up and lined in beautiful diagonal rows; hundred dollar bills bound with neat little ABA approved currency straps.

I couldn't even begin to guess how much was in there. Several hundred thousand, maybe a little more, maybe a little less. Joey Chill's long-lost drug money. Barrett's blood money.

I snapped the case shut and put it back in the safe and hung the nymph back up on the wall. Then I pushed the leather chair back in behind the desk, went quickly out into the hall and poked my head out into the alley. The cat was still there, licking its chops, giving me the Evil Eye. Otherwise the alley was empty. I went out and gave the cat a quick boot and it scurried off into the shadows.

Chapter Six

What I do doesn't take a lot of brains, and it doesn't take premonitions or deductions like you read in Sherlock Holmes or Hercule Poirot. Just a lot of guesses, some hard knocks, and plenty of legwork.

So that night I legged it right over to the Barrett mansion on Telegraph Road. I could have phoned, I guess, but I knew Barrett was in Sacramento for the weekend and I thought Melissa might be interested in what I'd found. At least, that's what I told myself, and I was hoping she'd believe it.

When I got there I pulled my crate up to the gate and got out. The gate ran on hydraulics, and it swung open only for those who knew the code. I didn't, but Melissa must have seen me there, because after a few seconds the buzzer buzzed and the gate swung wide open.

The driveway, which was paved in some sort of white material that might have been crushed oyster shells, led me to a porte-cochere. I got out of the car and walked up a flight of marble steps to the front doors. They had narrow leaded glass panels and a pair of ornamental brass knockers in the form of twin lion heads. I grabbed the ring that was hanging from one of the lion's mouth and used it to rap on the door. A few seconds later the door swung open and Melissa stood in the threshold like a succubus. It was after midnight, but Melissa Barrett wasn't wearing pajamas or a caftan. She was wearing a black strapless gown that flowed over her body like a silvery fluid and black stockings with a seam up the back. It might have meant that she had just gotten home, or it might have meant that she was just starting the evening.

"Nice knockers," I said, giving a perfunctory nod to the lions.

A little candle flame of a smile flickered among her straight teeth. "Come in, Mr. Brand."

In the big center hallway a chandelier was suspended from the high ceiling. I followed her through the hall and into a room twice as big as my entire apartment. I don't know what they call these rooms because I've never been in one, but there was a stone fireplace big enough you could walk into it and a wall of bookcases stuffed with stuff like Balzac, Zola, Stendhal, Schopenhauer, Engels, Strindberg, Swinburne, Rossetti, Wolf and Wheaton. The amazing thing about it was that all the books had the look of having been actually read and *reread.*

On the other side of the room were a leather sofa and a pair of red velvet Louis-the-something chairs. In the corner was a small walnut bar with a bottle of bonded bourbon and a half-empty glass. There was a large bubbling aquarium behind the bar with lots of multi-colored fish, but to tell you the truth, I wasn't a whole lot interested in exotic fish right then.

Melissa went over and sat on the edge of one of the Louis-the-something chairs. I sat in the leather sofa facing her. It put me too low down, so I got up and got the other chair and sat in that instead.

Melissa crossed her legs and let one of her little feet dangle there. It was a pretty foot. I could vaguely detect the painted toes through the black lace of the stocking and it made my lip start sweating. The way that foot was moving slowly back and forth was almost hypnotic, like an epigram in a story by Poe.

"Can I offer you something, Mr. Brand?"

The way she said it would have curled your mustache.

I took out a cigarette and rolled it between my fingers. I lit it slowly and waved the match until it went out.

"What do you have?"

Her voice was dry, cool, sardonic.

"Anything. Everything."

I glanced at the bottle of bourbon sitting on the bar.

"Got anymore of that?"

"Of course."

"I'll take it on the rocks, but not too many rocks. We don't want a shipwreck."

She stood up, expanded her body, and walked over to the bar where she poured the whiskey nice and slow, the way whiskey was meant to be poured. Then she turned around and I got a good whiff of her. What kind of alchemy, I wondered, could create a fragrance that could make reaction to the person wearing it so passionate, relentless and full of life? Just smelling her made me want to run around naked and beat on a bongo drum.

I watched her slink back into the chair and fold her right leg under her. She sipped her drink unhurriedly and kept her devil-green eyes right on me.

She said slowly, "Did you go to Robert's office, Mr. Brand?"

I looked at her and tasted my drink, she had built it just right.

"Yeah, I went there."

The corners of her mouth moved upward, though her eyes continued to evaluate. "And...did you...find anything?"

I took a good long swallow off my drink this time and stared at her over the rim of the glass. Her eyes never left mine.

I said, "Yeah, I found something. I found a big, fat .38 automatic. Do you know what that is, Mrs. Barrett? You point it at people and they fall down." I reached into my side pocket and pulled out the picture of Barrett's bimbo that I'd swiped from his office. "And I found this..."

I handed her the picture, leaned back, crossed one leg over the other and rested my drink on the top knee as I watched her.

Nothing changed in her face. Not a muscle of it moved.

I couldn't read this bird for the life of me, but something about her was making me dizzy with the dame. With all her troubles she looked good to stay away from, but I'm just an average gee, and brother, it works in reverse for us.

In a voice as blank as brick, I said, "Were you aware that your husband was also in possession of a large amount of narcotics? I found it stashed in a safe hidden behind a painting."

Something in her eyes changed that time and I saw her Adam's apple bob up and down as she swallowed.

"It's a Bouguereau," she said. "He got it at an auction in Amsterdam before the war. It's his favorite piece. And no, I wasn't aware of the narcotics."

Something in her face touched me this time. It was a look of deep requited weariness. She was sitting straight up, her knees close together. Her crowning black hair and small white hands on the arms of the Louis-the-something chair made her look like a tragic queen.

After a minute she threw back what was left in her glass. Then she got up, took the drink I didn't know I had finished from my hand and poured us another. On the way back she unconsciously flicked on the record player and the opening movement of Franz Liszt's *Dante Symphony* started playing.

She handed me my drink and sat down, folding her leg under her again. She was looking off into the fire, sipping her whiskey a little more ardently now. The big fireplace was a twitching, dancing thing that threw shadows across the room and touched everything with a weird, bestial light. It was too warm and I could feel sweat beading my upper lip. Under the charcoal grayness of my suit, my white shirt was sticking to me, and my tie was a block of warm rope around my neck.

I took out my deck of Luckies and offered her one. I stood over her and lighted it for her and she took hold of my wrist to steady the flame. Her fingers pressed harder than they had to and her eyes held mine like two green pools of warm water.

Her lips tightened into a narrow line, and for a moment she looked like an actress in a French movie.

"I don't know how I got into this mess," she said, her voice crusted with something like misery. "I guess I've always wanted to prove to everyone back home that I was something big, that I was better than the rest of them; but look what it's gotten me."

She held her cigarette pinched between her fingers and inhaled as though her lungs were in her toes.

I let her talk some more, not interrupting. She went on to tell me how she grew up in poverty in a little town up the coast called Isle Vista, with her domineering mother and a father who wasted his life away on gambling, whores, and whiskey. She would have told me more except for the inertia that overcame her.

"I just don't know what I'm going to do," she said, looking up at me with those eyes, and I almost got lost in the green world of them.

I heard the wind outside rattling the windows and Liszt was getting heavy now, gently thunderous.

"You see what Robert's planning, don't you?" She paused to take another toe-curling inhalation of her cigarette. "He's going to kill me and run off with this..."

She threw the picture of Barrett's bimbo on the floor.

"I don't know how I can help you, Mrs. Barrett," I told her. "Divorce is one thing. Drugs and guns are a whole nother bag of beans. I'm just a privately employed detective who makes his living babysitting the occasional celebrity and tracking down dead-beat husbands. Like I said before, maybe this whole thing is better suited for the boys in blue."

"Robert has friends who reach all the way up to the State House. I go to the police and an hour later I'd be dead. I'm all alone, Mr. Brand. You're the only person who I have left to trust."

The way she said it, half-pleading, half-come hither, half desperate schoolgirl—that's a lot of halves—almost turned me into Velveeta.

I stood up and took the smoking cigarette from between her fingers and killed it in an ashtray. Then I pulled her to her feet and kissed her on the mouth, with my left hand behind her head to hold it steady.

When I was done she opened her mouth slowly, and as she opened it, all the prettiness went out of her face and became a blank haggard mask on which rouge burned violently.

She moved toward me, very quickly, like a leopard, and one pretty fist caught me square in the jaw.

My head snapped back and a scalding wash of pain spread out all over my face and even down my neck on that side. The pain was livid, like an incision made across my chin. For being such a proper-looking thing, Melissa Barrett threw a mean right cross.

"I might be desperate, Mr. Brand," she screamed thinly. "But I'm not *that* desperate. I'm no pushover for broad shoulders and a gaudy smile."

I turned around and started walking out of that dungeon.

"Wait—!" she shouted.

I spun back on my heels and stared at her. The lush fullness of her lips had tightened into the faintest kind of snarl and her eyes were the carnivorous eyes you would expect to see in the jungle watching you from behind a clump of bushes.

And then something happened, something with electricity in it, like the white flash of a thrown switch when a new circuit is formed and then the current flows invisibly through another channel. I don't know if it was the whiskey, or the fire, or something else, but we both knew it was there.

I took her in my arms and pulled her close and she was warm and hard against me, her fingers biting into my arm.

This time she didn't pull away. She raised herself on her toes and her mouth touched mine lightly. The kiss was gentle at first, then fierce and hungry.

I ran my fingers down the small of her back and felt her body arch under them. We stood there in each other's arms and I could feel her heartbeat, tripping over itself in its haste to meet my own. Then she kissed me again, hard on the mouth to mean it.

I wasn't going to let her have all the fun, so I pushed her up against the wall and smashed her lips with mine. She let out a yip and caught her breath and hesitated for the briefest of moments, then she pulled my suit coat off and tore my shirt out of my pants and started working on the buttons.

The sling of my gun rack wouldn't come loose and she broke it. She threw the gun on the couch and was working her hands all over my chest, like someone learning to swim for the very first time.

I took that little black dress off her and got the bra off, too. Then I went down and got the slip and garter belt off. I slowly rolled a black stocking off of each perfectly formed leg and let them fall to the floor—slowly, like the last leaf from a dead tree.

Her skin was pale, except for the flush that dotted her face and neck like an exquisitely pedaled rose. Her breasts were small and the slenderness of her hips made her legs look longer than they actually were. She was a small woman. Petite, if you like those cute little words. I like them any way I can get them.

In a voice that was subdued, almost conspireatorial, she said, "Not here. Upstairs."

The hallway had a floor of black-and-white marble. Rising up from the center of the hallway was an elaborate double staircase. We did a little hopscotch on the floor's marble squares, her bare feet shuffling toward the vast curving staircase.

The house had an oppressive, muffled stillness. On the second floor there was an opened door. She stopped before it, her head averted as if she were having second thoughts, but there were too many little signs and hints of an unexpected closeness between us, as though our bodies had their own method of communicating now.

The bed was king-sized and covered with a peach silk spread. The windows were open and the air was warm and sweet and smelled like the summertimes of my youth.

I touched her legs, her thighs. I brushed my face over her flat stomach and she took my head in her hands and cradled it between her breasts.

"Be gentle with me," she whispered, moving slowly and heavily, as if under water. "It's been a long time since I've been with another man."

At first she whimpered like a puppy left out in the rain, but then her head swung up slowly, her black hair falling in her eyes, and all I could think of was a big cat, a great sumptuous black panther with luminous hair and a body of smooth skin that covered a plethora of rippling, deadly muscles and merciless ivory teeth ready to rip and tear.

"Now! Now!" she screamed out, digging her fingernails into my shoulders, until we melted together into a single warm wave, borne along by a long, divine rhythm that was both pleasure and pain.

♣♣♣

When it was over, we were lying on the big rumpled bed, naked and sweating, side by side, half-turned toward one another like the curves of a parenthesis.

I could smell her hair and her perfume and her sweat and I wished...Hell, I don't know what I wished.

I wished something.

After a while, I said, "Who was it I reminded you of?"

She looked up at me sleepy-eyed. "What do you mean?"

"That first day in my office—you told me I reminded you of someone."

A faint smile tugged at the corners of her mouth. "My father. He was just like you. A little rough around the edges, but he never let those edges get too rough. He used to call me his little 'Pumpkin Face.' That was his pet name for me. That was a special thing, from him to me. He'd bring his face down close to mine and say it low. He'd say he wondered where I got that pumpkin face of mine." She allowed another tiny smile to briefly appear on her lips, then it was gone as quickly as it had come. "But his gambling and drinking were eventually too much for my mother. She left him and we moved into a tiny one-bedroom apartment in Isle Vista. My father came around once in a while at first, but then the booze and the gambling and the whores snuffed him out. He lost his job, he lost what little money he had, and then finally, he lost his self-worth and any dignity that was left." The memory was an unwelcome one. Her eyes creased at the corners, and her mouth did too. "He ended up dying in some flea-bag motel in the muck of the Santa Ana stockyards."

I put my arms around her and held her there the best I could, until she fell asleep on my chest.

I tried to sleep, and couldn't. Everything that had happened was running through my mind like a gray web woven by a thousand spiders, and I started wondering what was going to come out of all this.

I tossed the questions around for a while and made everything but answers. Then the questions faded slowly to black and I finally fell asleep.

Chapter Seven

The sun was there in the morning, above the treetops and beaming in through the big bay windows. Melissa was sleeping next to me, curled up on her side of the bed, her face flushed with sleep and her black *Snow White* hair coiled all over her face.

I unpiled myself out of bed in a hurry and tried not to wake her. I didn't want to leave without saying goodbye, but I didn't know what time Barrett was due back from his meeting in Sacramento and I didn't want him catching me in *flagrante delicto,* so to speak.

I got dressed fast and when I put on my pants I discovered a roll of berries in my pocket that wasn't there before. I took out the money and counted it. Another five hundred. Melissa must have stuck it in there in the middle of the night.

I told myself it was her way of paying me for the coming week, but it felt more like she was paying me for sleeping with her.

I felt cheap, but the simple truth was, I needed the money, so I stuffed the roll in my pocket, leaned over the bed and kissed her on the cheek.

"See ya later, Pumpkin Face."

I grabbed the rest of my clothes and tiptoed out of the room. Her face was the last thing the light fell on as I eased the door closed and I took that away with me, the image of her sleeping face. She looked like an angel left here on earth by mistake.

I came out of the Barrett house and stood on the front stoop with my hat in my hand, holding it by the brim against my thigh. It was another balmy morning with the dew clinging to everything.

Out of sight, maybe around the corner, I could hear the sound of a sprinkler clicking in slow rhythms as it arched back and forth. Hell, the lawns around here didn't need watering, they were immaculate as any golf course.

I got in my scabrous Buick and drove off down the hill, wearing last night's clothes and Melissa's scent all over me.

I popped a Life Saver in my mouth, turned on the car radio and sang along with Bing Crosby's *"Aren't You Glad You're You?"*

I was thinking about the way Melissa had given herself to me so completely. Nothing held back. Whole. Body and soul. Everything. Her face was clear in my mind—the full red lips molded with a Rodinesque precision, the emerald eyes, the raven's hair that fell away from her face in great rich curls like clusters of black grapes.

On the car radio, Bing's song ended and the new Golden Boy, Frank Sinatra started singing *"Put Your Dreams Away."* I liked the tune, but thought Sinatra's voice lacked the vocal range to last long in the music business. He was just another one-hit crooner with blue eyes and a clever smile.

When I came down the hill Santa Rita was just starting to wake up, its bloodlines starting to push it along; the rush and chaotic sweep of cars and people swarming past me like the murmur of a distant sea.

I didn't want to go back to my apartment. It was dark, it was lonely; it was cold storage. It brought back a lot of memories—not of things I had done but of things I failed to do, wasted hours and thwarted days and opportunities forever lost because time had eaten so much of my life and I would never get it back.

But I had nowhere else to go, so I parked the Buick in the narrow alley; a ratlike passageway that went on and on between the tenement buildings and warehouses and seedy little bars.

The morning air was really starting to heat up now and I could smell the raunchy tide-smell of the ocean somewhere in the distance and the unmistakable stench of stale Chinese cooking emanating from the restaurant below my apartment.

It knew I was coming. My apartment. Waiting for me with a broad and ghostly grin. It knew I had nowhere else to go.

I went up the backstairs, went in; grabbed a bottle of Seagram's V.O. off the kitchen table, took a big swig and looked around the dump. It was not very big, not very clean, and certainly not very homey. I needed a dog or something.

I picked up the bottle again, took another pull, and started wondering what the hell a woman like Melissa Barrett saw in a man like Elston Brand, a boozy private eye with a drifting soap-bubble of memories. I started feeling pretty rotten about it, so I took the bottle with me into the adjoining bedroom—which was really just an extension of the kitchen—and fell on the bed. I threw around the pillows for a while, and finally fell asleep, a sleep that was short and full of sad and bootless dreams.

I woke up a few hours later and the heat was really revving up. I went over to the window and shut the blinds to keep the sun out, but that only made everything seem more dismal and bleak.

I went into the bathroom, took a hot and a cold, shaved my face with a thrice-used Gillette Blueblade, tried combing a certain amount of order into my hair, and got dressed. Then I locked up the place and went down to a hash house on Gambell Avenue where a lemon-shaped waitress who had been beautiful twenty years ago served me a stack of wheats, some greasy bacon, and the strongest black coffee she was allowed by law to serve. I plopped four cubes of sugar in it—with the Nazis defeated and the Japs on the ropes, sugar rationing had just ended and I still wasn't used to having as much as I wanted.

I ate quickly, left a decent tip, and got to my office at the Lafeyette Building a little after noon. On the way I kept dreaming of what it would be like to have a real office instead of a closet above Goldberg Bail Bonds.

I took the elevator up to the fourth floor and walked down the corridor to my office, my heels echoing hollowly in the empty space. I unlocked the door, turned on the lights and put the five bills Melissa had given me in the safe behind my desk. I still didn't feel too good about taking the money, in fact, I felt like a damn butter and egg man, but I'd been shatting on my uppers and keeping the bill collectors and bookies at bay for a couple of months now and the extra money felt damn good to have. I could pay off Bedbug in full now and still have a little left over to buy a few Prez Prada 45s for my Victrola and maybe a new pair of shoes. It'd been a while since I'd been able to buy a new pair of shoes.

I tooled around in my office for a while, then I grabbed the pictures I'd snapped of Barrett's bimbo out of the safe, found my hat somewhere, and waded over to the door. Switching off the light, I went down the four flights of stairs and out the lobby door, turned left along Ivar where my car was parked and drove over to precinct headquarters.

Frank was settled in his chair behind his desk, the Santa Rita Times in front of his face. I read the headline: MANHATTAN PROJECT TESTS FIRST ATOMIC BOMB IN ALAMOGORDO, NEW MEXICO.

A puff of cigarette smoke shot out from behind the paper. I sat on the edge of the desk and flipped down one corner of the paper with my pinky.

"Hello, Sergeant," I said, taking out a Lucky and sticking it in my lips.

"What do you want now, Elston?" Frank sighed. "You're like a depression. Always popping up when people don't expect you."

I took out the photographs of Barrett's bimbo and flopped them on the desk.

"Do you recognize this tomato, Frank?"

"What, no doughnuts this time?"

"Sorry, I forgot."

He looked genuinely unpleased.

"The girl, Frank. Have you seen her around before?"

He picked up the photographs and got a look on his face like a deer on the edge of the road when a truck comes unexpectedly around a bend. "Nice looking dame."

"A real Betty Grabel. Do you recognize her, Frank?"

He looked at the photographs more closely. "Yeah, I've seen her around. Name's Kitty Carlisle. She's a bump-and-grinder. Goes by the stage name Peaches."

"She ever get pinched?"

"Yeah, she fell once. Last August. She was new to the scene, but I remember she was a hard kid for her age."

"What did she get pinched for?"

Frank lifted his emaciated shoulders, then set them back down. "What else?"

"Solicitation?" I asked. "She's a pro?"

Frank nodded.

"What club does she work out of?"

"The Palomino," Frank said. "Down in the Berrytown Griffeytown neighborhood."

"Who owns the club?"

"Who owns all the clubs in that neighborhood. Salvatore Santucci."

"*Bedbug* Santucci?"

"You know him?"

"Yeah, I know him, and I've got the scars to prove it." I stuck a cigarette in my mouth and let it dangle there without lighting it. "What do you got on Bedbug?"

Frank killed his cigarette in an ashtray filled with snubbed butts. "We got wind a few months back of a prostitution ring that Santucci was running. Organized stuff, call girls, not street level. Real high priced. Cream of the pro-skirt crop. All of Santucci's dancers in his clubs work the lay on the side, but we were never able to pin the diaper on him. Everything's by referral. All the girls are clean as a peeled egg. They get a checkup every week and they take home good money, more than they can make waiting tables at the Brown Derby." He looked at me out of the side of his gray eyes. "This doesn't have anything to do with the Alderman, does it, Elston? You're not still sniffing around that drainpipe, are you?"

I stood up and slapped on my hat. "Thanks for the information, Frank."

His eyes got that squinty look. "It wasn't my intention, Elston. Next time bring more doughnuts."

Chapter Eight

Like most metropolitan muck heaps in America, the city of Santa Rita has two facets. On the one hand, it's a respectable world of order and propriety; on the other, it's an underworld of crime, vice, and murder; a world of jungle violence and darkness, of sharp-clawed betrayal and fanged merit, where scruples and principles are just other words for weakness and naivety.

There's an old section of Santa Rita known on maps, town-records, and the like, as Berrytown Griffeytown, but is in fact spoken of simply as "Old Block 20." A twenty-block sprawl of peep shows, grind-houses, pawnshops and gambling dens. A place inhabited by a milieu of low-grade Mafiosi, black pimps, Latino gangsters, "rough trade" homosexuals, trench coat-clad perverts, and thrill seeking squares. You'll never find Berrytown in any tour book brochures of the Golden State.

I got on Muldoon Street and followed it onto Eighth. Then I turned left on Oilwell Road, weaving in and out of traffic, watching things all around me.

Club Palomino was on the corner of North Fourth Street, in the very heart of Old Block 20. I had seen the place before, but I had never been inside. It was like a hundred other night clubs all over the city, with red tube neon letters blinking:

CLUB
P
A
L
O
M
I
N
O
LIVE NUDE GIRLS

The Palomino was no haven for a piker. A drink was two dollars a throw, and the *couvert* four. If a b-girl sat down with you, your drink or hers was three dollars a throw, and her own drinks were doctored with nine parts Canada Dry. A "clip-joint" built back in the early '20s when Santa Rita was still the blushing virgin sister of Los Angeles, where the b-girls were famous for hustling men and when you got drunk enough, they'd rob you blind.

I shook my head at the hat check girl and kept my hat on my head. On the walls were mural paintings of dramatic scenes from Shakespeare. Those parts of the walls that had no murals were painted a dark, brooding red and adorned with silk drapes in various shades that complemented the colors of the multicolored tiles on the floor.

There was a tiered orchestra stand at the back where a drummer was singing out of the side of his mouth, *"Through the black o' night, I gotta go where you go;"* and a large stage with a red velvet curtain where the paid entertainers sweated out their three-a-days. Red was the predominant color of the place.

As the magenta lights focused on the still-closed curtain, there was an aura of murmuring expectancy in the house, then the curtains finally rose into the flies, and a chorus of ten girls in what I can only call abbreviated costumes—masses of red feathers and garter belts—started coiling and uncoiling in a long sinuous line, their bare legs flashing in soft white, very nude flesh to some number that had nothing to do with any story line. I couldn't catch many of the words, but the song had something to do with everybody getting together and having a wonderful time. The men in the audience were certainly having a wonderful time. They leaned over the railing in the loges, whistles and catcalls punctuating the music.

Still thinking of feathers and garter belts I went up to the long bar set into the far wall where an iron-jawed brick of a bartender with a handlebar mustache looked at my twenty-dollar suit and asked in a not-too friendly voice if I was from the Health Department. He looked like he could break my back with his pinky.

Sticking out my chest, I said, "Where's Bedbug?"

He knotted his Neanderthal brow and it looked like he was trying to figure out a tricky problem in Chinese algebra. "What you want with Bedbug?"

I reached into my shoulder holster and eased my .38 out, placing it on the bar as simply and discreetly as possible.

"Look here, you little two-tongued dago," I said. "I'm in a bad mood tonight. I haven't shot a man in almost a week. Tell me where I can find Bedbug, or you just might be that man."

"You a cop?"

"Private. A shadow. A shamus. A flatfoot. A gumshoe. A dick. I'm all eight minutes," I said, smiling at him, only it didn't really have much to do with smiling. "Now listen to me, you're pushing my patience and I'm not a patient man to begin with. I've got business with Bedbug."

He looked at me like he wanted to use my face to wash his car.

Finally, he said, "Mr. Santucci is at his table over there in the corner."

I turned around and yes, there he was—sitting at a solitary table all the way at the back of the room. A glow of red from the weak footlights barely outlined his head against the back wall.

He was surrounded by his gorillas Jimmy the Weasel and Leadpipe Leo and a handful of other suntanned Mafiosi. Bedbug gave off a powerful alpha vibe that all the other men at the table deferred to without hesitation. There was no question who the boss was.

I walked through the crowd to the table.

"Hey, fellas," I said to Jimmy and Leo. "How's life in the zoo?"

They looked up at me and growled.

Bedbug was meticulously molded in a gray suit, polished Italian shoes, purple shirt with white buttons, tie undone for exact sharpness and airiness. A man has to be confident in his masculinity to wear a purple shirt.

Bedbug wrinkled his brow at me and smiled. "Elston Brand! What are you doing in this neighborhood?"

"Slumming."

He smiled, with his mouth, not his eyes. He was a taut little I-tie with small, neatly chiseled features and dark eyes framed by long black lashes. He had shiny black hair, and his hands were slender and long. His face was clear as a cameo, almost without hardness. He had a way of looking at you, from the side, glancing away then back, that made it seem as if he was looking at you from two directions at once.

He scratched his chin with the nail of his little finger, which he had grown more than an inch long.

"Do you have my money, Elston?"

I took out the money Melissa had given me and slapped a lovely sheaf of green down on the table. They had big, beautiful numbers in the corners and I hated parting with them.

Bedbug took the bills and folded them tenderly away. It was like watching someone steal your girlfriend away from you.

"The debt *was* a grand, Elston, but with interest—you still owe me two hundred. You got another week to come up with it." He grinned widely, exposing a gold tooth in the front of his mouth. "What did you do anyway, win the lottery? You want to place another bet on the ponies?"

"I gave it up for Lent."

"It ain't Easter."

"It don't matter, the last horse I bet on was wearing snowshoes."

He showed me some of his gold teeth again. "Nobody quits, Elston. They just stop for a while."

On stage a tin voice over the public address system broke the spell of the drumbeat. "And now—what every man in Santa Rita has been dreaming of—the Palomino's own Candy Meadows."

The curtain glided up and a clattering of handclaps greeted the woman standing in the footlight glow. The girl on the stage was not overly pretty. Her nose was thin and straight, and the planes of her face were not irregular.

Her drawing power was her body; curved and flamboyantly sexual, it thrust arrestingly against the sheath of scarlet satin barely covering it.

"I'm looking for a girl, Bedbug."

His teeth were a potpourri of white and gold in the slash of his smile. "Ain't we all?"

"Yeah, but this one's special. Ever hear of a girl named Kitty Carlisle aka. Peaches? I heard she's working for you."

"Everyone's heard of Peaches. She's one of my new intellectual *ectasiates*."

"Ectasiates?"

"Strippers."

"When did you get a thesaurus?" I asked him.

His nostrils seemed to flare out a little. "I'd be careful of that mouth of yours, Elston. I could have one of my boys put a foot in it."

"Tell me about Peaches."

I got the gold-toothed smile again. "She's a riser. Bright, clean, smart. What everyone's looking for."

"She working tonight?"

"You just missed her. Her shift ended about an hour ago."

"Where does she live?"

"You know Ulysses?"

"I read the book."

"Huh?"

One side of my mouth smiled. "Never mind."

"She lives on Ulysses Street. At a place called the Pedicord. What do you want with her anyway?"

"A case I'm working on. I heard she got hooked up with the Alderman. You wouldn't know anything about that, would you, Bug?"

I knew he didn't like being called Bug, but I couldn't help myself.

"If I did, I wouldn't tell you, Shamus. And the name's *Bed*bug."

"Sure it is. How'd you get that name anyway? I always wanted to ask."

He smiled heartily across all his face and said, "When I was a kid just off the boat from Sicily, the first girl I took into the sack I bit her in the ass."

"Charming story," I said. "Maybe someday you'll be able to tell it to your grandkids."

Chapter Nine

The building Kitty Carlisle lived in was an old one, converted half a dozen times from whatever had been its original role in life. In the small forward atrium there was an intercom box on the wall, with a speaker grate and plastic buttons with apartment numbers next to them. I ran my fingertip along the names under the buttons. The name next to 3-C was written on a strip of masking tape KITTY CARLISLE, but before I could put my finger to the buzzer a fat drunk slob and a middle-aged floozy with dyed red hair stumbled out, holding the door open for me.

Kitty Carlisle lived on the third floor, and it was a walk-up. I picked my way up the stairs and by the time I got to the third floor I was blowing like a bull moose. I stopped at the head of the stairs, to get my wind and my bearings, and looked around.

A wine-colored carpet crept down the middle of the hallway and a red fire door loomed at the back. It smelled like all apartment hallways. It wasn't just an odor. It was something that moved; something warm and fluid.

I walked down the faded runner and stood in front of 3-C, knocking twice before I heard the languid tap of heels come toward the door and stop.

I knocked again, this time a little harder, and heard the bolt being sidled back. The door opened a crack, maybe enough to stick a finger or two in it, if you were dumb enough to risk losing a finger or two. In the crack I saw a little eyeball staring back at me.

"What do you want?" the eyeball asked.

"My name's Brand. Elston Brand. I'm a private investigator..."

There was an afterthought of hesitancy; then the chain-head slid off its groove. The eyeball disappeared momentarily and the door was pulled open.

Kitty Carlisle held onto the door with one hand on the jamb, sort of leaning on the hand, running her left thumb across her lower lip and looking me over from floor to hat. Not the way most women look at a man, but the way most men look at a woman.

"You're a private dick?" she asked, in a voice that had left innocence a lifetime behind.

"Uh-huh."

"Do you have a gun someplace on you?"

"Probably."

"You ever shoot anybody?"

"Only those that deserved to be shot."

"Well, then, enter and be sanctified," she chortled. It was an oddly strange sound—hollow, deep in her throat, not feminine at all.

She was wearing a sweeping red evening gown that seemed to start halfway down her waist and matching go-to-hell lipstick. There was no fullness to the dress. It clung, and under it there wasn't the slightest indication of anything else.

She had the kind of body that would make a statue drool. Long legs and ample mammary glands and a belly that had just the right amount of bulge to it.

She looked cool and sarcastic and I bet she snapped a mean garter belt.

I stepped through the door and followed her inside. It was a nice place, furnished on an allowance, with a leather sofa and loveseat and an expensive-looking combination radio-phonograph. A half dozen Frank Sinatra records were scattered on the carpet.

"What did you say your name was again?" she asked, her eyes shadowed by mascara and experience.

"Brand. Elston Brand. What's yours, honey?"

"No, it's Kitty."

"Can I call you Peaches?"

Something you might call a smile threw a shadow around her experienced mouth.

"So, the private dick has done his homework."

It was hot inside the little apartment and the little red dress she was wearing left little to the imagination.

"Make yourself at home," she said. "I just got off work and my dogs are yapping. I'll just go slip into something a little less comfortable."

She pirouetted in her high-heeled pumps, lifted her hair off her neck, and asked if I'd help her with the zipper on the back of the dress. Who was I to deny her?

As she was walking out of the room she slipped the dress down over her hips and it fell to the floor like a rose pedal. She was playing it for all it was worth, and buddy it was worth plenty.

A few seconds later she came out of a back bedroom wearing a white nylon babydoll, pink slippers with kitty-fuzz on them and white stockings as sheer as Venetian lace.

"Ah-h, that's better," she said, moving like a lazy cat toward the loveseat.

She sat down and crossed her legs deftly, the skin showing in a generous sweep above the stockings, and there was just a touch of blonde peach-fuzz on the well-muscled thighs.

"Do you have a cigarette?" she said, her voice coming in a dry weary whisper. "I forgot to stop at the five-and-ten on my way home from work."

I reached into my coat, pulled out my deck of Luckies and handed her one. She took it in her long fingers and slowly put it between her lips.

She had smooth, bare arms. She folded them so that the line between her breasts became deep and high. I felt the sweatband of my hat grow tight and itchy.

As quick as a ferret, I said, "What do you know about a guy named Robert Barrett?"

For a second she looked like I had just told her the Japs had invaded San Francisco.

She jerked and puffed on her cigarette. "Never heard of him."

"Never heard of him, huh?"

"Nope."

She unfolded her legs, stood up, and started slithering toward me. She was the type of dame that made a guy feel like he walked into a propeller; the type of gal that was no stranger to the sight of a stranger's underwear.

"You're a good-looking guy for your kind of racket," she said with heavy-lidded eyes. "You can tell so much about a person from such simple things as looks."

"And what does my look tell you?"

"That you're one of those self-indulgent gumshoes you see in the movies who think about nothing but his guns and his dames. I'll bet you do a thousand sit-ups every morning to keep your stomach hard. How does someone become a private dick anyway?"

"I saw an ad in the back of *Picture Show Magazine* and sent away for my license. You interested in becoming a private eye?"

"I didn't know they existed, except in books or movies—or else they were sleazy little men snooping around bedroom windows."

"I'm not above snooping around bedroom windows."

"You're a real smooth talker, ain't ya, Mr. Brand? I bet you don't have much trouble with women, do you?"

"Every guy has trouble with women," I said. "My problem is with women who call me Mr. Brand. Call me Elston."

"Okay, Elston," she said, letting her arms crawl up my sides, her hands going to my face, then lacing them behind my head. "I'll call you anything you want me to call you."

I was harder than the Hope diamond, but I let the touch of her practiced hand slide off me like orange juice off a duck's back.

I said, "So, Robert Barrett? What do you know about him?"

She closed her eyes and moved her hand toward my lips. "Enough about this Robert Barrett you keep talking about. Why don't we get down to business—" She started unbuttoning the yoke neck of her gown.

"I don't pay for sex," I told her. "My business is information."

"Everybody pays for sex," she said, adding a couple extra syllables to "sex," ending it with a hiss like a snake in a chicken coup. "The only difference between sex for money and sex for free is that sex for money usually costs a lot less."

"Is Barrett one of your clients?"

A cunning light shone in her eyes. "Who I screw is *my* business, mister."

Suddenly I was very tired of Kitty Carlisle, tired of the game we were playing. There was a dry sour taste in my mouth that made me want to spit, a buzzing around my head that pulled my lips tight across my teeth and brought the voices back in my ears.

"You've got about as much morals as an alley cat, sister."

"Some guys like alley cats. I can be an alley cat, Elston. I can be anything you want me to be."

I don't make it a hobby to deck many dames, but some dames are just begging to be decked, so I decked her in the mouth.

Her head jerked back and her eyes were knifed with pain. She brought her hands together in a sudden unconscious gesture. Her bottom lip was split wide open and blood was spilling out onto the white babydoll. It looked like a kid had taken a purple marker and drew all over her lips.

A second later she was smiling again. "So, you like it rough, huh?"

"Usually I like it anyway I can get it, but you're a hundred-dollar-an-hour whore trying to sell her wares for a penny, and you're wasting my time trying to figure out why."

"Fuck you, private dick!"

"I'll take a rain check, sister."

I walked out of there wondering what Robert Barrett saw in a doxy like Kitty Carlisle, beyond the obvious optical reasons, that is.

I was still wondering about it when I caught the glimpse of something streaking through the shadows of the hallway toward my skull just before the blackjack hit me on the side of the ear and almost smashed the consciousness from my body.

I swung back from the blow, feeling hot pain spread into the entire right side of my face.

Staggering, I collided with the banister, and then I got hit by the blackjack again.

This time I went down onto the floor and the next thing I knew someone was sitting on my back, feeding me to the wine-colored carpet and I felt my nose being pushed all the way into my head.

I tried to move, but couldn't.

"Stay out of this, Brand," I heard someone say. "If you know what's good for you, you'll stay out of this!"

My face was jammed into the carpet again. This time I felt my nose shatter and pretty soon all I knew was blackness, severing me like a guillotine, and the scene had never existed at all and everything became a badly remembered dream.

♣♣♣

I woke through a red fog of pain. I could hear words all run together and felt someone's breath, foul with a stale whiskey stench, being blown upon me.

"Are you okay, buddy? Did you fall down? Had a bit too much to drink tonight, have we?"

I opened my eyes and saw the fat slob and the middle-aged floozy with red hair standing over me. I almost screamed when I saw the floozy's face so close to mine. It was portly and round and painted up with a bad make-up job, like a drunken weekend suburban birthday clown.

"Do you need an ambulance?" the fat guy was asking me.

I rolled over on my back, making guttural animal noises and feeling the blood from my broken nose drip into my eyes.

I tried to sit up. That wasn't such a good idea. The whole smelly hallway started spinning like I was about to disappear into the Bermuda Triangle.

"Take it easy, buddy," the fat guy said. "We need to get you to a hospital. Your face is pretty broken up there."

I swallowed stale blood down my throat and managed to miss the walls standing up. My lips felt hot and huge and one of my teeth felt loose in its socket. I was pretty sure my nose was broken.

I staggered down the hallway toward the stairs.

"Hey, where you going, mister?" the floozy called after me in a voice that reminded me of Shakes the Clown.

Chapter Ten

The beating I had just taken should have sent me straight to the Emergency Room, or at least home to bed to hide beneath the covers. There's nothing that cleanses your soul like getting the shit kicked out of you. But I needed a drink and my appetites were up, so I decided to make an assault on an Old Scratch Amber and on Angie, my favorite bartendress instead.

It was dark and dead inside the Red Carpet and it reeked of sour mash and broken promises, but it was like a second home to me.

Angie was behind the bar, buncoing some drunk with an oversized bindle of twenty dollar bills that he seemed more than willing to part with. Angie was the type of dame that could talk a cat into barking.

I grabbed a stool and started bleeding all over the bar.

When Angie saw me she poured me an Old Scratch without me asking for it.

"My, God, Elston! What happened to you now?"

I patted the back of my head where I'd been sapped and winced. "I got into a boxing match with a kangaroo."

"Silly. There are no kangaroos in Santa Rita. You better let me take a look at your scalp."

She took out a first-aid kit from under the bar and probed around the lump on the back of my head. If she had found a hole to stick her finger in back there, I wouldn't have been at all surprised.

She squirted a little Bactine on it and wrapped it all up in adhesive bandage until I looked like a poor man's version of Boris Karloff.

"Cured?"

"Momentarily," I said. "What do I have to do to put it on a permanent basis?"

Her teeth showed in a grin when she looked at me. "Put it on a permanent basis."

"I've tried."

"Maybe not hard enough."

"I'm hard enough."

"Don't be vulgar. You look like road kill, Elston. Pretty soon your face is going to be nothing but a piece of bone with a strip of skin hanging from it."

"You know what they say in the movies, it's only a flesh wound. Ah, you're worried about me."

"A little. And that's a lot for me."

"When are you going to marry me, Ang?"

"You know I'm not the marrying type," she said crushingly, lighting a Chesterfield with a great click of her lighter. "Did you know that marriage is the number one cause of divorce? If we got married it would be like eating Corn Flakes for breakfast every morning. Day after day, the same old thing. We'd get bored."

"I'd settle for night after night."

"Who'd pay the bills?"

I lit a cigarette of my own. "This type of conversation should exclude practical considerations, Ang."

"Who's being practical? We'd last about a week."

"Yeah, but it would be an interesting week. Someday I'm going to make you change your mind."

"Someday," she laughed; her breath hot and sweetly boozy in my face.

"I can't wait around forever," I said, feeling like one of the boys of Pointe du Hoc storming Normandy. "I'm getting old in my young age."

"You're not that young, Elston."

"I'm not that old either."

I finished my beer and got up. The drunk at the other end of the bar was staring at me.

Angie blew me a kiss from across the room and I went out into the hot wet California night and drove home.

Chapter Eleven

The next morning was warm and sticky and so was I. There was too much going on in my head to stay in bed. I crawled under the shower and let the cold water bite into my skin. When I dried off I shaved, brushed my teeth and went to my office and the only person in the building was a quack doctor in the hallway and he had to look twice to recognize me. It was a hell of a feeling. You live in a city for ten years and are still unknown to your neighbors.

I got on the elevator and took it up to the fourth floor and went into my office. Southern California was in the middle of the hottest summer in years and the radiator in my office was busted, permanently roaring away, the metal getting red-hot in places, making it hotter than a Scandinavian steam bath.

I opened the windows and turned on the radio and spent the next couple of hours sweating and getting caught up on some paperwork. My desk was next to the big windows, dusty and ready for repossession, like everything else in the room.

Babs Gonzales, Tadd Dameron, and Dizzy Gillespie were bopping on the radio. At noon, the national newswire announced that an American B-25 bomber mistakenly flew into the Empire State Building, damaging the 78th and 79th floors and killing thirteen people.

Ten minutes later there was a knock on the door. I turned off the radio, grabbed my .38 out the desk drawer, stuck it in my pocket and opened the communicating door.

The door swung open and an aircraft carrier with arms walked in. He was tall and blocky, suggestive of great physical power even tailor-made clothes couldn't conceal, with pronounced buck teeth, a flat nose, close-set eyes, and a stare that might remind one of a character out of a Bram Stoker novel. He could have played center for the Los Angeles Dons football team. Hell, he could have been the entire offensive line.

I kept my hand on my .38 the whole time.

"Can I help you with something, Mighty Joe Young?" I asked, but the aircraft carrier didn't speak.

Another guy walked in behind the aircraft carrier and it took a few minutes for me to register that the other guy was Robert Barrett. I almost choked on my tongue when I finally realized who it was.

"Hello, Mr. Brand. We haven't met, but I know all about you."

"Is that good?"

"It helps."

He came in and helped himself to the customer chair in front of the desk. He sat down in it and made himself comfortable, like he'd been there a million times.

"Make yourself comfortable," I said.

He had on a smart tan double-breasted suit that probably cost more than the rent for my office, which I was six months behind on.

Barrett smiled and when he did his teeth were as white as the snow on top of the Santa Rita Mountains.

"Do you know who I am, Mr. Brand?"

"No," I lied.

I'm a great liar when I'm scared. If there's one thing I've learned in this business, it's this: if you have to lie, you should do it quickly and as well as you can.

Barrett looked as if he didn't believe me. "My name is Robert Barrett," he said, his voice smooth and rough at the same time. "I'm the Alderman for Los Angeles County." He was proud of it.

I nodded at the aircraft carrier standing over his shoulder. "Who's your pet?"

"That's my assistant, Dominick," Barrett murmured with just a tilt of his head.

Dominick kept staring at me like he wanted to take a bite out of my neck.

"Your assistant, or your heavy?" I asked Barrett.

"Let's just say Dominick's job is to watch over me, to make sure nothing *distasteful* happens."

I played it with an even bigger smile and said, "Anyone as important as the Alderman of Los Angeles County certainly needs a protector. Do you have a leash for him? He's making me nervous. It's a city ordinance to keep all pets on a leash, you know?"

I thought even Dominick might get a kick out of that one, but neither of them so much as cracked a smile.

"Please, Mr. Brand," Barrett said, manufacturing a cursory chuckle that fell about a hundred feet short of sincere. "Let's cut with the pleasantries."

"Is that what we were doing?" I asked, feeding my face a butt.

Barrett winced. "Must you smoke? I'm allergic."

"I must," I said, blowing a smoke ring in his tan face. I didn't give a duck's butt if he was allergic. "Now, what did you come here to see me about, Mr. Barrett? Surely not to tell me I can't smoke in my own goddamn office?"

I was playing it as tough as I knew how. If he came here to kill me for messing around with his wife, I preferred he get it over with.

"I came here this afternoon to discuss something of importance with you, Mr. Brand." For the first time he looked sincere and not like he had more important places to be and more important people to see. "What kind of name is Brand anyway?"

"It's Scottish," I said. "My family's motto is: Either Peace or War. The Brands were descendents of Olaf the Black and were noted for their ferocious and war-like character." I had no idea where I pulled that one out of, but Barrett seemed to buy it.

"That's very interesting."

"Yes, it is, but you didn't come here looking for a genealogy lesson either, did you, Mr. Barrett?" I stood up and went over to the metal filing cabinet, where I pulled out the office bottle. "Care to dip the bill a little?"

I figured a guy like Robert Barrett didn't abide this early in the afternoon—or abide at all—but he surprised me.

"Sure, I'll nibble one."

I poured a couple of ponies into two thick chunky glasses.

"Does your pet want one?" I said, looking up at Dominick.

"Dominick doesn't drink," Barrett said.

"Of course he doesn't."

I handed Barrett his glass. Then I sat down behind my desk and leaned back in the rickety chair.

Barrett sipped his rye and made a little face. He had a mouth made to kiss babies with.

Then he said, "I want to employ your services, Mr. Brand."

I damn near spit out my drink. I would have, but I didn't want to waste good whiskey.

"I beg your pardon?"

"I said I want to hire you."

I tilted my head. "If you don't mind me asking, Mr. Barrett, where did you hear of me?"

He looked at the scarred wreck of a detective in front of him, surveyed my wrinkled suit and drooping smile, and did his best acting in an attempt to hide his lack of confidence.

"You came recommended as a man who can get the job done and who can be trusted to keep his mouth shut. You've got the sort of reputation I want in a private detective. A good reputation goes a long way."

"Who recommended me?"

He put a touch of firmness and authority into his voice, like that was supposed to impress me. "You came highly regarded by a few police friends of mine."

Yeah, I believed that like I believe you should draw into an inside straight. It fit like a glove fits a foot. I had to struggle to keep my face straight. Any police friends of his surely hated my guts.

I cocked an eyebrow and asked, "So, what do you want me to do for you, Mr. Barrett? Run a few wire taps, shake down a couple extortionists?"

He wiped his lips nervously with the back of his hand and I thought I saw real pain in his eyes.

"I believe my wife is seeing another man," he said desperately. "I'm sure in your business, Mr. Brand, you've come across this type of thing numerous times, but I implore you to have some decorum. I love my wife very much. I want you to follow her for a few days. Routine stuff, I believe. Take some pictures, let me know what you find."

Suddenly my face got very hot and I had a hard time catching my breath.

"Are you all right, Mr. Brand?" Barrett asked.

"Yeah, it's the damn radiator. It's busted." I took a desperate pull off my drink. "What makes you think your wife is cheating on you, Mr. Barrett?"

"Does it matter? I just know, that's all." He paused long enough to get in another nibble of his own drink. We were putting them down like two old Army buddies. "But I need proof. That's where you come in."

I knew it was unethical in my business to accept retainers from opposing factions, especially since I was sleeping with one of them, but as Humphrey Bogart once so casually tossed at Elisha Cook following a colorful display of tetchiness: Things are never so bad they can't be made worse.

Why couldn't a P.I. have two clients at a time? Sure, it'd never happened to me before, but it came at a point when I could use all the help from Franklin and Jackson that I could muster. What the hell, the way I saw it, you only live once, or twice.

"I get a hundred a week," I told him. "Plus expenses."

Barrett looked at me like a scientist would look at a bug through a microscope. Then he took out a wallet that was not quite as big as a bale of hay and spread out ten century notes like a tight poker hand, and put them down on my desk. They made a flat sound that was pleasant to my ear.

"There's a thousand dollars there, Mr. Brand. That should be more than enough for a retainer. You'll get another thousand dollars when the job is completed. Do you accept the arrangement?"

Did I accept the arrangement?

A thousand dollars was sitting on my desk with a promise for a thousand more and this goose just asked me if I accepted the *arrangement?* I thought about pocketing his grand and breezing off into the sunset to grow old on a beach somewhere. I could leave Santa Rita for a while, find a nice little beach in some underdeveloped country, sip fruity cocktails, and look at all the young slave girls with hot spurs and a bucket full of sin.

But something inside my thick skull was telling me that it didn't add up. It was like trying to stick a square peg in a round hole. The whole thing threw a loop in Melissa's claim that Barrett wanted to kill her. Why would he hire a private eye to spy on his wife if he planned on feeding her to the fishes? It just didn't make any sense. Nothing was making sense. I started wondering if there was indeed another man. Other than me, I mean. I felt the bile rising in my throat. It had already gotten to the point where I couldn't stand thinking of Melissa with another man, as crazy as that sounds. The thought was an ugly one, so I got it out of my head pretty quick. She was mine now. I was ready to kill for her, if that's what had to be done.

"Do we have an arrangement, Mr. Brand?" Barrett said again.

He wasn't giving me much time to think about it, but it never occurred to me to refuse the money. Very early in my career I learned an important theorem: When someone puts that kind of money in your hand, you close your fingers around it and stuff it in your pocket.

I picked up the cash and almost licked it.

"Yes, Mr. Barrett, I believe we have an *arrangement.*"

Chapter Twelve

As soon as Barrett and his gorilla took it on the heel and toe, I picked up the blower and had the operator put me through to Melissa.

"We need to talk."

"So, talk."

"Not over the telephone."

We made plans to meet at the Red Carpet.

I got there early and went in and bumped gums with Angela at the bar.

"How's the memory, Ang?"

"Forgetting is the hard part." She tapped out a smoke and stuck it between her lips. "Been busy?"

"Running errands."

"Two nights in a row? I missed you, Elston. You ever miss anybody? I mean, really miss them? It's a drag. If I start to feel too sorry for myself and turn into a lush or something, it's your fault."

"You won't," I told her.

"I won't? I'm just one of your favorite bartendresses in all the world, is that it, Elston?"

"One of my favorite."

"Uh-huh, I know the type. If I refused to serve you, you'd hate my guts." She tapped the ash from her cigarette out in an empty beer bottle. "Your face looks a little better."

"Yeah, I haven't fought any kangaroos lately."

She gave me the rag end of a smile. You've never seen a smile like that. Then the smile went dormy, and she said, "That pimp Bedbug Santucci was in here today looking for you. He said you still owe him two-hundred dollars."

"If he comes in again, tell him we're square, will ya, Ang?"

"I thought what's-his-name ran this part of town?" Angie asked. "Mickey Binnaggio."

"Not no more," I said. "Bedbug took it over."

"How'd that little slug ever do it?"

"It's called free enterprise, Ang. The last anyone's seen of Binnaggio he was short two fingers and an eyeball. Word on the street is he hightailed it to Phoenix and is living in a nursing home."

Angie's eyebrows furrowed with a proprietary anxiety. "Ah, Elston, why do you get yourself involved with these kind of people?"

I shrugged. "It's what I do. To live like me you got to be able to give a punch and take a punch. You've got to have a stomach like a distillery. You've got to be early for everything except bed."

"Why don't you quit the P.I. business and get a real job, Elston?"

"And do what? Get a job in a factory or behind a desk, being stifled by dry rot and dying every time that second hand goes slowly round the clock?"

"It's better than getting your head kicked in or getting yourself killed."

"Sometimes I get to do the beating up, Ang."

"Yeah, well, sometimes I wish you'd keep your hands to myself."

At that moment Melissa walked in, wearing pointy black shoes and a black silk dress with a v-neckline. Her legs were long and alive and she was coming out of that little dress like a tube of Colgate Dental Cream.

Something about her made me warm under my clothes. She was built like a goddess should be built and her eyes said that she was good when she should be bad.

Angie's eyes went dim and straight when she saw Melissa. "Who is *she?*" her voice low and almost choleric.

"She's a client of mine."

"A pretty client of yours. Maybe I should be a client of yours, but I doubt that I could afford you. I'm being nosy, huh?"

I smiled and pinched her nose. "Yeah, but it's such a pretty nose."

Angie smiled back. "While you're talking to your *client,* I'll put on higher heels."

I stood up and nudged my chin to the booths in the back and Melissa followed me.

"So what did you need to see me about?" Melissa asked, easing into the booth like liquid.

I dropped my voice to a hoarse whisper. "Your husband came to see me today."

Her eyebrows, which were the most mobile feature in her face, shot up alarmingly.

"*What?* What did he want with you? He doesn't know about...*us,* does he?"

"No. At least, I don't think he does."

"What does he want then?"

"He wanted to hire me," I said, keeping my eyes on her. "He wants me to follow *you* around for a few days. Snap a few photographs. He thinks you're having an affair."

A beautiful frown wrinkle appeared briefly between her eyebrows now. We had a short staring contest, and then her stare turned ugly and she said, "How much money did he give you?"

"A grand up front," I said. "Another grand when I finish the job. That's a lot of cornflakes, baby."

She stared down at the table, as if there was an answer there she didn't quite have. Then she laughed lightly, way down in her throat, and leaned on the table and cupped her chin in her hands.

"I'm hungry," she said.

It wasn't exactly the response I had in mind.

I didn't know what to say. So I said, "We could eat here, but it might kill ya."

I suggested we drive over to Redondo Beach for some real food. Plus it would give us a chance to get out of Santa Rita for a while and be by ourselves. Santa Rita isn't a very big town. As it was, we'd have to be a damn sight more careful than we'd been, which hadn't been any. No one would recognize us in Redondo Beach.

We slipped out of the booth and headed for the door. As we passed the bar Angie narrowed her eyes at me and I gave her a look back.

"See ya later, Alligator," she said.

"After while, Crocodile."

I shoved Melissa out the door to where my Electra was waiting. The car was so old Moses could've driven it across the Red Sea, but Melissa didn't seem to mind.

"I'll drive," she said.

I threw the keys at her.

She took the wheel like a sixteen-year-old who's just got her license and I was gripping the armrest all the way down to Redondo Beach.

"What's the rush?" I asked, but she ignored me.

We pulled in at a little Chink place I knew of called the Nankin. It was down an alley off East Benson Avenue, away from the tourist crowd. We went in and found a booth well away from the bar. The place was designed to look like you were in Beijing, with big balconies, dark corners, and goldfish-filled aquariums.

The booth was padded thickly with foam rubber and the gloomy lighting made it almost impossible to see across the room. The waiter, a little Charlie Chan look-a-like with a wide smile, appeared magically out of the darkness and handed each of us a greasy menu that was bigger than Melissa's entire head. Holding the gigantic menu in front of her she looked like Alice in Wonderland at the mad tea-party.

"Do you still have the Wanderous Punch?" I asked Charlie.

He nodded his little head emphatically. "Certainly, certainly! And to eat? Maybe Moo Goo Gai Pan, or Lion's Head Meatballs?"

I shook my head. "Nah. How 'bout a steak? You gotta couple plain old steaks back there?"

He looked like I had just insulted his mother back home in China. "Sure, you want steak, we got steak."

"Thanks. And how 'bout those drinks?"

He nodded sincerely and left for the bar, but I thought I heard him whisper something like, "Stupid Americans," along the way.

When he reappeared he was holding two tall glasses the size and shape of a flagon. The Wanderous Punch was a giant, tasty, multi-liquored concoction, not intended for amateurs and often surprising even seasoned drinkers like myself with their potency.

A few minutes later our steaks came. They were fat and bloody, just the way I like them. I thought Melissa might protest, but she ate with wild abandon, like it was her last meal. I looked at her petite figure under that little black dress and wondered where she put it all. She must have had one hell of a metabolism. She looked more lus-cious than the oversize T-bone she was gnawing on.

We ordered another round of Wanderous Punch, raised the tall glasses in a silent toast, and sipped the top off them. When we finished our drinks, I flipped the bill and we left. On the way back to town we got to what was really on our minds, and it was her that brought it up:

"Elston, you know what this means, don't you?"

"What what means?" I asked.

"Robert hired you to clear his own conscious," she said. "He wants you to find me with another man so he can kill me. What he doesn't realize is that *you're* the other man."

I looked over the car seat at her. I didn't want to say this, but I had to say this.

"There aren't any others, are there?"

The pitch of her voice changed. "What are you talking about? I admit that I'm no angel, but I swear to you, there's no one else. Jesus, Elston."

"I'm sorry."

The closer we got to Santa Rita, the hotter and darker it got. The lights made a milky halo over the rooftops and the glittering ray of a searchlight at the casino in Casa Canejo prodded about among high faint clouds.

"It's weird," Melissa said, gripping the steering wheel and staring off into the night.

"What's weird?"

"How things in life turn out. From one moment to the next, you never know what's going to happen. If someone had told me when I was a little girl in Isle Vista that this was the future, I would have laughed. Sometimes I wish I never had Robert's money."

"Sometimes?"

"I've gotten too used to it," she said. "A girl has to live, you know? And it isn't always as easy as it looks. As soon as I turned eighteen, I left home. I guess I've always been a dreamer. I was born dreaming and I dreamed my life away. Do you know what it's like when a girl leaves home and goes out on her own? Let's just say she doesn't have any difficulty meeting men. For the first time in your life you're grown up. You're on the loose. You have an apartment, you are your own boss, you don't have to ask anybody for anything. Or, that's what you think. But you're not *really* independent. Nobody really is. You can get just so high and no higher. And so a girl can make a mistake, marry a wealthy man, looking for something that isn't there. Security or whatever." She paused and a darkness fell over her. "I don't think I could go back now even if I tried. Besides, Robert would never let me go back now."

For a long minute neither one of us spoke. She drove with her head leaning back against the seat staring out the windshield at the night. She plucked the cigarette from her lips and blew a stream of smoke at the windshield. Her dress was crawling up over her knees and I could see her tanned thighs over the elastic band of her black stockings.

Cautiously, I gathered the material of her skirt with my fingers until the hem was above her waist.

My hand squeezed the warm flesh above her stockings. She squirmed in the seat and her legs made a beautifully obscene gesture.

I closed my palm on her thigh with a sudden warmth and urgency and felt the bare flesh there, smooth and muscular.

When my hand went higher up on the inside of her thigh, she gripped the steering wheel more fiercely and her head rolled on the seat until she was looking at me. She started to say something and closed her mouth over the words, then she squeezed her legs together gently to keep my hand there. A stiff breeze had worked its way down from the Hollywood Hills and there were gray patches of fog swirling in groups, slowly slinking past like boundless souls on the run.

"We could run away together," I told her.

"Where would we go?"

"Anywhere. What do we care? We'll ditch this town and blow. Just blow."

"And live on what?" she said. "How long would we last with no cash? A month? Maybe two? Until we hit a hard time and I remember how easy it was to do nothing and live high. I gave Robert almost three years of my life. Do I write them off now? Throw it all away and say to hell with three years of my life? You don't get that many years, Elston. I don't want to throw three years of my life away. Besides, we could never run away. Robert would find us no matter where we went."

"We could take some of his money, your money, and we could go away. Find a little island somewhere and change our names. Spend our days lying in the sun and our nights rolling around in the hot sand..."

Her smile was a thin wet crescent now and her words were a deep, hot breath. "That sounds nice, Elston."

"We could do it," I said.

We didn't talk about it anymore. We laid a few miles behind us without saying anything to each other. By the time we got back into Santa Rita it was a little after midnight. The traffic signals at the corner of Water Street were turned off for the night; only the intermittent blinking of the yellow caution lights at the four corners of the intersection lighted the lost, drifting plumage of fog.

Melissa's car was in the parking lot of the Red Carpet where she had left it.

She got out of the Electra slowly and I slid over to the driver's side. She stood beside the window, with the warm wind sweeping her black hair and molding her dress against her body.

Slipping her hand through the open window, she laid it lightly on my wrist. Then she took a step back and looked at me like she was seeing me for the last time.

The wind blew her hair in an arc around her head, dancing around her shoulders, rising and falling as if it had a life of its own. She put up her hand to it. She had small hands, the wrists no bigger than a child's. Then she turned and started walking toward her car.

"Think about what I said," I called out to her.

She looked over her shoulder.

"Goodbye, Elston Brand."

Chapter Thirteen

For the next few days I watched her, determined to probe the situation she was involved in—and yet protect her at the same time. I still wasn't completely sold on the idea that Barrett was planning to kill her, but I wanted to be sure nothing happened to her in the meantime. And Barrett was paying me to keep an eye on her anyway. The way I figured it, I was baking two cakes in one oven.

In the mornings before the sun rose, I drove over to Telegraph Road and parked my car in the shadows of the big tamarind tree. I watched the house with my Kodak propped on the dash, drinking too much black coffee, smoking too many cigarettes and listening to Bob "Shamrock" Shannon on KLIT radio announcing that the Japanese city of Toyama was destroyed by B-29's.

Barrett always left early in the morning around 7:30. The house remained quiet and dark after he left, until Melissa woke up, usually around nine or nine-thirty. She spent an hour reading the newspaper and fixing breakfast. Then she drove over to the health spa on Cahuenga Boulevard. It was one of those five-star resorts designed to keep you and me away. I sat in the car and watched her sweat through the big windows. I remember when I was a little kid back home in Battle Creek, I'd play detective all day, pretend I was Steve Midnight or Sam Spade or Horace Dorrington, pick someone out of a crowd and follow them around all day. It was sort of like that now.

An hour later Melissa would get in her car and drive back up the hill. When she got home she'd kick off her sneakers and slip out of her work-out clothes, shower, then spend an hour indulging herself with Dreyer's Rocky Road ice cream. In the evening she had a light meal alone—Robert rarely made it home for dinner—then she spent an hour primping and pruning and pouring herself into black evening gowns split high up on her right leg and scooped low over her chest. The high-heeled stilettos were almost a necessity.

Then she got in her little red Aston Martin and sped down the hill toward the Delaney Park Strip and the nightclubs that line 5th Avenue. Her favorite was a place called Latitude 61. She danced all night; jive, jive and more jive, with a little bit of Lindy and Jitterbug thrown in. On each side of her stood pretty dimpled boys, like smiling cupids.

The ginks fell all over her, buying her Manhattans, Mojitos, and Martinis, showing their polished smiles, whispering in her ear, trying to rub their hands all over her. I wanted to kill those slimy Lotharios. I wanted to take care of her.

I wanted to be her boy. That's all I wanted for Christmas, brother.

At the end of the night she always left the clubs alone. Like Cinderella, she'd hop in her little red chariot at the first stroke of midnight and zoom up the hill, through the gates to her castle where she'd go in and leave her high-heeled slippers at the door and slip out of her party dress and slide into bed next to her sleeping husband.

The routine was the same every night.

♣♣♣

On the fourth night I wanted a little dirt with my evening, so I pointed my car toward the waterfront. I felt like spending some time in my own neighborhood for a change; maybe even get a little gowed-up, so I decided to head over to the Red Carpet for a fill of the giggle juice.

But a couple of coffee-and-doughnut guys had different plans for me.

I adjusted the rear-view mirror and saw the prowl car, with its cherries flashing in the buzzing evening heat.

"What the hell is this all about?" I wondered, pulling my heap over to the side of the curb.

The prowl car pulled in nicely behind me and a big bull cop and his partner stepped out. They walked slowly up the side of my Electra and I took the beam of Bull Cop's flash in my eyes before he lowered it.

He rapped on the window with his knuckles. They looked like miniature baseball bats.

I rolled the window down and gave him my best Beau Brummel smile.

Bull Cop turned out to be a flatfoot I knew vaguely from the Fifth Precinct named Updike; a rough and woolly breed of nail-eater with a pouched, florid face, little round unblinking eyes, and a bad toupee that moved at a different tempo than he did. He was dressed in the shapeless, baggy suit some manufacturer in Hoboken makes especially for plainclothesmen.

His partner was about my height, though skinnier, with a black waxed mustache and an ivory face with pimples for eyes and a lipless tobacco-stained mouth and a half-moon scar across his chin.

In a voice that had the volume and command of the entire brass section of the Boston Pops, Updike said, "Get out of the vehicle, Brand."

I got out. Our eyes met. It was not love at first sight.

"What's the problem, Officer *Uptight?*" I asked.

His eyes bulged and the veins stood out in his neck.

"It's Up-*dike!*" he said, and before I could say "How do you do" he punched me in the gut.

I coughed and thought I tasted blood, but before I could cry "Police brutality," Updike hit me again.

I stood there, cramped over, puffing air like a big fish.

"You wearing iron?" Partner asked me. He had Rasputin-like eyes that seemed to take everything in at once without moving at all.

"I'm legal," I told him.

Updike reached out and got hold of my right arm above the elbow and triggered the spring release of my shoulder holster and my .38 popped out barely tugging my lapel.

"Nice gun. You got a ducat for that piece, bo?"

"I said I'm legal," I muttered, reaching slowly into my wallet to take out the license. "I'm an op."

"Let's see your ticket."

I took out my bona fides. They had my picture on it and a thumbprint and two official-looking countersignatures that said I was a licensed private investigator by the State of California.

Partner had his fingers on the butt of his gun the whole time, watching me slowly and intently. His uniform was wrinkled but his boots were new and shiny; the overhead lights reflected in them and made me dizzy.

"What's this all about?" I asked.

"We got a call about a vehicle loitering in the neighborhood," Partner said. "Vehicle has been seen parked up on the side of Telegraph Road for several days now." He looked at my poor car disgustedly. "An old beat-up sky-blue Buick Electra, just like yours."

"A vagrancy call?" I almost laughed. "You pulled me over for a vag charge?"

Updike started running his meaty hands all up and down on me, looking for another gun or perhaps a chiv, but I didn't care who the hell he thought he was, he had no right running his paws on me for a vagrancy charge.

I gave him a shove just to let him know I was still there.

He got a surprised look on his face and grinned. His dentist must have been tired waiting around for him.

"You wanna play tough, huh, Brand?"

"I'll play it any way you want to play it, Uptight."

"It's *Updike! Updike!*"

He reached around his waist, pulled out a pair of silver bracelets and tried snapping them on my wrists. We didn't even know each other that well and here he was, already giving me jewelry.

"Get your flippers off me, flattie!" I said, pushing him away.

Updike raised his rather large fists, and said, "How would you like a poke in the button, smart-guy?"

"How would you like a foot in the ass, fatso?"

This time Partner hit me. Right across the face with his service revolver. I fell to the cement, blood trickling down my cheek. Now I had a deep gash under my eye to match the bruises on my nose.

Partner let out a weird, maniacal laugh and kicked me in the ribs. He didn't talk much; hell, he didn't talk at all. He just let his feet and fists do the talking.

I spit blood onto the pavement and looked up at him.

I heard Updike tell Partner: "Hit him again, Georgie. Make him like it!"

Partner gave me a couple more kicks to the ribs and head and I was flopping all over the pavement like a guppy out of water.

In all the commotion, I barely saw the back door of the prowl car swing open, but it did, and a tall cop in plain rags stepped out. A vague silhouette under the street light.

He was wearing a dark Borsalino hat with a gay print band and a long flogger over his plain rags. He yanked his collar up and stepped over toward us, a trail of cigarette smoke following him like a train.

"Break it up, quit that nonsense," the flogger said, with no more fanfare than the winking red lights on top of the prowl car.

At the sound of Frank's voice, Partner ceased his mad stomping of my head and torso.

"C'mon, Frank, let us work him over a little bit more," Updike pleaded.

Frank was eating a Marlboro like it was candy. He smashed the cigarette out on the ground with his shoe and lit another one. He had his hands shoved down in his pockets and he was watching me roll around the ground with eyes that were half shut.

"I tried to tell you that you didn't know what you were getting yourself into, Elston."

"Call your dogs off, Frank," I said, or tried to. What came out was more of a breathless wheeze with no consonants.

"Why have you been parked out in front of the Alderman's house for the last week, Elston?"

My shoulders hunched into a shrug and I tried pulling myself off the concrete.

"I told you I was working a case."

Frank drew on the cigarette cupped in his hand. His tie, which looked like it had been tied around Roosevelt's first term, swayed down near his crotch.

"Who are you working for, Elston?"

"I can't tell you that, Frank. I'm on a confidential lay. Word gets out that I canaried to the coppers, I'll be out of business. My clients pay me to get information, not to give it."

He leaned against the door of the Electra, folded his long arms, and rubbed both eyes with the heels of his open hands. He needed a shave. The gray stubble on his chin made him look old and mean.

"I used to like you, Elston. But you're gonna force me to do things I don't want to do."

His half-hearted threat slid off me like milk off a duck's back.

"There's nothing here that tells me my case has anything to do with the Santa Rita Police Department," I told him. "If it does, then I'll have to tell you who my client is. But right now, I don't have to tell you anything."

Updike grinned like a split watermelon. "You're a real bright boy, ain't ya, gummy? If you get any brighter we'll have to call you Sunny. You're a worthy contender for Mensa."

"What's that?" I asked. "A place for broads who have problems with their periods?"

Frank was starting to lose his composure. "Are you going to tell me who you're working for, Elston?"

"Nope."

"I can make you tell me."

"You're tooting the wrong ringer, Frank. I'm just trying to make a living here."

"I could send you over to the clubhouse."

"On what charge?"

"Let's take it alphabetically. Complicity, conspiracy, collusion. Not to mention obstruction of justice."

"I'm not obstructing anything. I'm just doing my job, and getting my face kicked in for my trouble."

"You're treading on dangerous ground, Elston. I warned you once not to snoop around Barrett's drainpipe. Stay away from him. And stay away from that bump-and-grinder Kitty Carlisle." Frank threw the cigarette that was glued to his face in the gutter. "Get out of here. Go climb up your thumb."

"Can I have my gun back first, Frank? I've grown quite attached to it."

Frank nodded and Updike reluctantly handed me my .38. I packed it away in the oiled leather holster under my arm and crawled back behind the wheel of my heap. In the rear-view mirror I watched Frank and Updike and Partner get back in their prowl car.

After they drove off, I sat there for a minute, while a little finger began poking at my mind, trying to knock something into it that should have already been there.

I thought Frank and I were friends, but someone high up was forcing him to sick his dogs on me, and I wanted to know who it was.

Chapter Fourteen

I drove west on Water Street, crossed the avenue and got back to my kind of people again.

When I got to the Red Carpet warm rain was coming down like Babylon.

A flood of light and a thunder of jazz from the jukebox rushed out as I went in.

The place was tight with soggy men and a handful of giffers looking for an easy lay. I took a seat at the bar to be close to the liquor and to be close to Angie. She was wearing red shorts and a red halter top. Soft and well-rounded like summer roses.

"What's the wire, Ang?"

She gave me a shrill half-sigh, half-moan that sounded like her voice was cracked.

"It's no fairy tale, mister."

I fished for a smoke and pulled a wreck of a butt from my pocket. "That's okay, baby, 'cause I'm no prince."

She saw my face for the first time and I thought she was going to throw up.

"There you go, Elston, getting yourself beat up again. You look like the south end of a horse going north."

I glanced in the mirror behind the bar and was shocked by my own reflection. I looked like Victor Frankenstein's favorite plaything gone horribly awry. All I needed were bolts sticking out of my neck.

"We all have bad days, Ang," I told her.

"Tell me about it, I'm having a bad lifetime."

She looked like she needed a Lucky.

I offered her one and she took it eagerly. She tapped the end of it gently on the edge of the bar, leaned forward for my light, then stood up and settled behind the bar again.

"Listen, beautiful," I said. "I'll make a bet with you. Bet a quarter I can kiss you without touching you."

"Okay, I'll take that bet. Just don't bleed on me."

"Get ready. This is going to be a cinch."

I leaned across the bar and kissed her on the lips several times.

"You lose!" she said. "You touched me when you kissed me."

I shrugged. "Here's your quarter."

She poured me another beer and I lit my hundredth cigarette of the night and for the next hour I sat there by myself pouring oat sodas down my throat like a dehydrated legionnaire.

About five beers later the door swung open, letting all the soaking wet in with it.

I turned my head briefly to look who walked in and almost choked on my beer when I saw Robert Barrett and his tattooed gorilla Dominick standing there.

All of a sudden my beer tasted lousy.

Barrett came in, took off his jacket, snapped it once to get the top layer of moisture off, and took the swivel chair beside me at the bar.

He ordered a Scotch. Dominick hung back by the entrance, his big eyes scanning everything like a loafer in a country store.

"These guy's friends of yours, Elston?" Angie asked me from behind the bar.

It made me feel warm and fuzzy all over to have her watching my back, but I saw the clumsy square butt of a .38 bulging out of Dominick's coat and I didn't want anything ugly to happen.

I told Angie to set 'em up.

She poured front-shelf Scotch into a relatively clean glass and set it in front of Barrett.

"Want anything, Mac?" she said to Dominick.

He didn't say anything back. I was starting to wonder if Dominick had a tongue.

"He doesn't drink," I told Angie.

She stared at Barrett who was sipping his cheap Scotch slowly and bitterly.

"Want me to throw him out, Elston?"

I smiled. "No thank you, Angela, he's got enough trouble drinking your booze."

Angie left us alone and went back to the giffers at the other end of the bar.

Barrett cocked his head at me and smiled his thousand-watt smile. "She's quite a woman."

"The cat's pajamas."

He tried sipping his Scotch again. "How have you been keeping yourself, Mr. Brand?"

"Perfectly ducky. How'd you find me here?"

"You're not hard to find."

I didn't know what that was supposed to mean, but I let it pass.

He paused to look me over pretty carefully, and then said, "What happened to your face?"

"I slipped in the shower."

His eyes had a sort of foxy eagerness. "You have to be more careful, Mr. Brand."

I took a sip of my beer. It still tasted lousy.

"What do you want, Barrett?"

"I came to see how you were coming along on the case."

"I thought I told you I'd report to you when there was something to report."

"It's almost been a week," he said. "Does that mean you haven't...?" His voice went low and tight, like somebody was holding his windpipe and he had to force the words out of his mouth. "...does that mean you haven't seen Melissa with another man?"

"I've seen her with lots of men. Every night she goes out to the clubs and does the Jitterbug. But she always goes home alone. Listen, Barrett, I'll be honest with you. I'd like out. This whole thing really doesn't call for a private investigation. I'd suggest a marriage counselor I know down on Sunset. He could hook you up on the cheap."

"Look, Brand, I'm paying you a large sum of money. I'll decide what this calls for. I heard you were a good man. You stick with it. I'm satisfied you'll do the job." He looked a little pale, or just tired. I couldn't tell which. "I'm leaving for a few days," he said after a long pause. "I have to go to Sacramento on business for a few days. My line of work often takes me away."

Sacramento again. I wondered what was really in Sacramento. My face was stiff with thought, or with something that made my face stiff. It could have been the booze I'd been downing for the last hour or it could have been the thought of Melissa alone again for a few days in that big house of hers on the hill.

Barrett cocked his head and moved his eyes over my face.

"If you need to contact me, telephone Dominick. He'll put us in touch. He has my complete confidence."

I looked over at Dominick and smiled. "Mine too."

Barrett finished his Scotch and stood up to leave. Then a thought hit me like a sucker-punch.

"When will you be back from your trip, Mr. Barrett?"

He flicked me a sharp glance. "Next Tuesday. Why?"

"No reason."

"Goodbye, Mr. Brand," he said abruptly, heading off toward the door. "If you need anything, please contact Dominick."

Dominick gave me a quick, half-empty smile that might have meant nothing—or anything, then he wandered off after his master.

I sat at the bar again, ordered another beer and a shot of sour mash to keep it company. I didn't like seeing Barrett, because every time I saw him, I thought about him touching Melissa. I didn't like to think of him anywhere near her. It made me hate him a little, because after that night with Melissa I thought how unfair it was that a hefty old politician like Barrett should have something so precious while I spent my nights alone.

I straightened up at the bar, slammed the booze, and told Angie to keep it coming. Life is cheap as a private dick, and a lot of eyes turn to drink to make it a little less mind-numbing, and I'm no better than the average gumshoe. I could start my drinking in earnest now. Why not? No one was worried if I made it home alive; or if I was drunk and sick in some alley. I felt like the prodigal son, except I had no one to go home to. I felt mean, mad, and blankety-blank. I was lonely and aching for Melissa all over and I wanted to get drunk. The last time I checked there weren't any laws against it.

I ordered a couple more rounds and then the whole room started spinning. I stood up, gripping the lip of the bar, and slapped a Lincoln down for all of Angie's trouble.

"Are you okay, Elston?"

"I've been known to be soberer," I slurred. "Wait—I take that back."

"You drink too much, Elston. Only frustrated people drink so much, and only lonely people are frustrated."

I saw her lips moving but I couldn't hear what she was saying. I didn't want to anyway.

I slapped on my hat and stumbled out into the stinking rain; a thin, dirty mist like a lace shawl that's been worn too long between washings.

A streak of lightning cut across the sky with thunder rolling in its wake.

I wandered around the street, bumping into walls and trash bins before I found my car, but when I got in I found that it had somehow shrunk. I couldn't fit behind the wheel and I had to scrunch over, with my knuckles hanging over the dashboard.

The road had two center lines and I almost ran over something lying in the gutter that might have been half-human. I don't know what time it was when I finally made it home. I looked at my watch. It said five o'clock but it seldom told me the truth. No amount of changing the battery had ever done it any good. It had been given to me by my ex-wife back in '37, along with a pile of debts I was never able to pay.

I went up the back steps and into my apartment, took off my shoulder holster and left it lying on the floor. The apartment was dark and smelled of burnt popcorn, cheap whiskey and sweat socks. I kept thinking about making love to Melissa. Then I kept thinking about Barrett making love to Melissa and it made me even bitterer.

I was already drunk, but that never stops drunks from drinking more. I stumbled over to the ice box, and when I opened it, the burst of light from inside hit me like a flash bomb going off. I took out a bottle of cheap whiskey that I kept in there just in case I was ever bitten by a red-backed shrew.

I took the bottle and a chunky glass and stood by the open window in the living room and stared ruefully out at the rain and the carpet of lights downtown.

I used to like this town a long time ago. When I first got here Santa Rita was just a bunch of small wood-frame bungalows on the outskirts of Los Angeles. A big, dry, sunny place where people used to sleep out on their porches along the beach, but then the riff and the raff started drifting down from the City of Angels, and now it was just another neon-lighted slum surrounded by a sea of strip clubs, liquor stores, and bowling alleys. A lot of the old places I once knew are long gone.

After another snort of whiskey I lighted a cigarette and watched it burn between my fingers. I was getting too old. Thirty-nine going on fifty and I was still slumming through the dirty streets of this two-bit town.

I finished my drink and poured another. There were no red-backed shrews lurking around the apartment, but you can never be too careful.

Chapter Fifteen

When I woke up the next morning my stomach felt lined with broken green bottle glass and I had to belch about every five seconds, and when I belched it made the glass jiggle. It wasn't a hangover; it felt more like an alcohol-induced stroke. The left side of my face was numb and the other side was swimming in a cloud of carbonation. One of those moments of bad ambiguity that make you tell yourself you'll never drink again, even though you know you most certainly will.

Drink, drink, drink. Smoke, smoke, smoke. Schmuck, schmuck, schmuck.

My lungs hurt, my nose hurt, my eyes felt like they had knives in them, and my throat felt lined with quills from all the cigarettes I had smoked the night before. I stared at my distorted face in the bathroom mirror. It looked like an uncooked pot roast.

I thought a hot shower might help. It did, but just a little. Standing beneath the water I let the needle streams beat into my upturned face. The steam made me sleepy. With an involuntary yelp I twisted the faucet to cold and forced myself to stand under the pelting needles of ice for a full two minutes. My whole body felt like it had been doused in liquid nitrogen.

By the time I stepped out of the shower I was feeling half-human again. At least I felt like having another drink and a butt without choking over the thought. I dried myself off with a relatively clean towel, wrapped it around my waist and went into the living room to get another bottle, and when I did, Melissa was standing there.

She was standing in a slice of shadow through the blinds, like something conjured up too quickly and I didn't know if I was dreaming or not. Everything about that moment fitted in with the unreal, dreamlike existence I had been living since that first day I met her.

She was wearing a tailored trench coat that was belted around her waist and shiny black stilt-like boots.

"I came to make love to you," she said, her face so completely shadowed that no expression showed on it.

She pulled the belt off the trench coat, revealing a white garter belt and white stockings and nothing else.

"Robert's gone to Sacramento. He left this morning and won't be back for three days."

There was nothing giddy or impulsive about her intentions. She had thought things through carefully; had made a conscious choice.

She didn't smile. I didn't smile. We just stood there staring at each other like a couple of sloppy-faced puppies.

Then she took several steps toward me, the black leather boots clicking on the hardwood floor.

"I came to make love to you," she said again, grabbing the towel from my waist and yanking it off.

At that moment I would have walked on fire for her, would have engraved her name on my bicep with a rusty nail; would have slit my wrists if she merely asked. I would have fallen at her feet and kissed each one of her pretty little toes and played This Little Piggy if she wanted me to.

For a second I thought that was what she wanted me to do, but instead she grabbed the back of my head and sunk her teeth into my lips so deep I could feel the blood spurt into my mouth. It was running down my chin when she took me to the bedroom and told me to sit on the bed.

She put one of her legs on the bed, unzipped the boot and threw it on the floor, running her long tapering fingers over her thigh, unfastening the catch of the stocking off the garter.

Slowly stroking downward with her fingers, she rolled the stocking off the thigh and down the ankle and over the foot.

I thought I was going to come apart at the seams like a dime-store baseball. I couldn't take it any longer. Without waiting for her to undo the other stocking I grabbed her violently and held her neck firmly so she couldn't move away.

I cursed her in a whisper. "Damn you."

She pressed herself closer. "Why?"

"Because I think I love you."

She brought her lips down on mine, snapping at them with her tongue. Our hands roamed over each other like blind people searching for a door. I put her down on the bed and she looked up at me. Then I grabbed her thighs, pushed them apart. She threw back her head and bit her bottom lip which was stained with my blood.

It was hot in that tiny room, and we were sweating from every pore, twisting around in the sheets, nipping at each other like rabid dogs, and for one delirious, pulsing moment, the rest of the world outside my tiny dark apartment dissolved into nothingness.

Chapter Sixteen

I sat in bed smoking cigarettes, listening to the thunder and watching the lightning outside my window while Melissa slept softly beside me. Every time I stole a look at her it felt like my whole world had changed.

When the sun finally peeped into the windows, I slipped my arm under Melissa's neck and kissed her. She yawned, a wide, childish yawn and rubbed her fists into her eyes.

She woke up with me kissing her and we stayed in bed all day.

That night we drove over to her house to get a few of her things. She was going to spend the next few days with me until Robert came back from his trip to Sacramento.

We drove through the Hollywood Hills and got on Telegraph Road. The sky was red in the west, dying the streets under it as though somebody had spilled a bottle of Heinz ketchup on them. It was good to be alive on a night like this.

At the end of Telegraph Road a fox darted out of the woods, shooting across the pavement, its little crimson body taut, hugging the ground, as if it thought it could sneak by unseen. I had to step on the brakes to avoid hitting it. I wondered what that fox was up to. Probably sneaking around, hunting for someone's kitty cat to snatch.

When we reached Melissa's place we went through the gate and up the winding white driveway with the wet shrubbery all around us. I pulled in under the big front entrance and waited in the car as Melissa went to get her things.

As I waited I lit a cigarette and smoked it to the nub. Then I lit another one. The guy on the car radio announced that the U.S. had dropped the second Atom Bomb "Fat Man" on Japan, destroying part of Nagasaki.

So much for the war, I thought. Pretty soon all the boys would be marching back home.

About a half hour later, Melissa came out of the house carrying a smart overnight case with the initials M.S. on it.

M.S., I noticed, not M.B.

She got in the car and I asked her what M.S. stood for.

"My name," she said. "My maiden name. Melissa Sparrow. Like the bird."

Melissa Sparrow.

I liked it because it meant she wasn't Melissa Barrett anymore. At least for the next couple of days.

We drove down the hills and stopped at a Red Owl supermarket in Westwood Village, just down from the Strip. I went in and bought a fresh bottle of Seagram's. Then we drove back to my apartment and threw off all our clothes and that was the last time either one of us was dressed for the next three days.

We spent the whole time in bed, making love the way the Romans used to. We never left the apartment. The world outside ceased to exist and time moved as slow as a wet week.

When Tuesday morning finally reared its ugly head, we cursed the day and refused to get out of bed, but we both knew we had to. Robert was due back from Sacramento sometime after noon.

"Pin your diapers on, honey," I told her. "You've got to go back."

We got dressed and I kissed her goodbye and she went down the rickety staircase to the alley where her little red Aston Martin was waiting for her. She got in sullenly and I watched her drive off and there was a feeling inside me like a little kid has when Christmas morning comes and passes and all the presents have been unwrapped.

♣♣♣

The next day passed unbearably. It felt strange not having Melissa around. For the first time in a mainly self-sufficient life I was all at once so terribly alone. I could still smell her presence all around, lingering on in the form of a *Channel No. 5* perfume cloud.

I thought of her having to go back to Robert. I wondered what she would do if he asked her to make love to him. It was burning me up inside just thinking about it. The thought of him touching her made me want to kill something.

He would be home now. They'd be sitting down to cocktails and dinner. He'd ask her how the last couple of days were. She would lie and tell him that they were *quite boring without you, dah-ling!*

Life is nothing but a goddamn series of lies, one piled on top of another. But that's exactly the way people want it to be nowadays.

I went into the kitchen and tore the plastic off a new bottle of whiskey and took it with me to the window where I stared out at the dark clouds forming over the rooftops of the warehouses.

Thunder rumbled across the sky and for a second there was a dull glow over the city.

Something wet smacked against the window. Then another. Then a whole spew of fat raindrops.

The walls creaked and the rain scratched against the windows, and I sat alone with my bottle of whiskey, hearing words in the wind, rising and rising in a haunting crescendo: "Kill him! Kill him! Do it! Kill him!"

It was an easy out, a way to solve all my problems, a way for me and Melissa to be together.

But it was still murder, and I couldn't kill someone in cold blood, no matter what it meant.

Or could I?

Chapter Seventeen

The next night I decided to tail Kitty Carlisle a.k.a. Peaches. Something in the back of my craw told me she knew more about Barrett and the stash of cash and H hidden behind the Bouguereau.

It was a bad mistake. One of those moments in life you wish you had back to do all over again.

It was a hot, moist night in which the air clung to you like the memory of a bad lover. I scraped the wheels of my Buick at the curb across from Kitty's apartment a little before 8:00pm. An hour later she came out of the building wearing a red raincoat like Little Red Riding Hood. She scanned the street, then walked down half the block to her car. It was one of those little foreign jobbies with a glistening paint job that reminded me of the color of a gun. I spun the Electra around and followed her.

She turned left on Cajalco Road, past the Delaney Park Strip, skirting the Santa Rita Cemetery toward the deserted South Park Freeway. The sun was sinking in the west, and red clouds glowed like flames over half the city.

With a lopsided moon hanging on the other horizon, I followed her dim red taillights as she drove south toward Deluge Point and Corona Del Mar State Park. Ten minutes later she turned off on a one-lane road at Potter's Marsh and continued west toward Turnagain Arm.

I followed her through the winding road and the still woods with those taillights periodically vanishing like summer fireflies.

A few minutes of that and we turned inland, into a hollow at the end of a gorge and then up on the high ground and after a little while down again and up again.

Halfway up the ridge overlooking the silver-blue waters of Pescadero Bay, the taillights turned off into the driveway of a small cottage. It was a gravel road with woods on both sides, and completely deserted.

I went up past the first turning, and parked in the ditch after turning the car around. There was nothing but the sound of breeding cicadas and the croaking rumble of distant bullfrogs. A weather-beaten sign nailed to a tree said: "NO TRESPASSING."

I switched the lights off altogether. Then I climbed out of the Electra and made my way toward the cottage. Below was darkness and a vague far-off sea sound.

Kitty Carlisle's car was parked in front of the foot of the cottage with its lights off. The cottage seemed deserted, except for the smoke curling from its single chimney. It looked as if someone had designed it for an Edward G. Robinson movie, right down to the pile of cordwood and the double-bitted axe on a chopping block beside the front porch.

I moved up the driveway. Everything looked peaceful, normal.

A light flicked on in a back room and a shadow moved across the cracked, yellow blind. I crept along the side wall and stood on my tiptoes, peering into the window.

The vibrating white light of a gasoline lamp on the table gave the room an ugliness as precise as a bad photograph. In the corner of the room there was a small stove, a table, and two cots, one tumbled, one made up as neat as a pin.

Suddenly Kitty Carlisle appeared against the square of light. There was someone in there with her, but I couldn't see who it was. Kitty was standing with her back to the window, blocking my full view of the room and the other person with her.

A voice floated out from the shadows:

"I don't want to force you into doing anything, Kitty—"

"You're not—"

"It's just—"

Silence.

I listened. The wind and waves from the ocean in the distance made it hard to hear their muffled voices through the window.

I listened:

"You want a cigarette?"

"Sure."

Someone exhaled.

"Thanks."

More silence.

Then the voice again:

"It's just...I don't think the timing's right. I think she's getting suspicious..."

"What?"

"I think she suspects something—"

"What makes you think—"
"It's just a feeling."
"Has she said—"
"No."
"Then how—"
The shadow behind Kitty started moving slowly toward her, the face still a mask of semi-darkness, and all I could see was the gray elbow of a coat sleeve.

Kitty still had her back to me, almost against the window. She didn't move and she didn't say a word as the shadow approached her.

The shadow picked up a paring knife from the table.

Kitty's voice had risen gradually to a high, thin monotone.

"What are you doing—"

There was the sound of a blow on flesh.

Kitty uttered a loud groan, modulated by the half-formed syllables of broken words. The shadow's right hand holding the small, bright knife rose above Kitty's shoulder and descended into her.

She screamed, sprawled backwards across the wall, and rolled heavily onto the floor. A thin red line appeared in the cheek below the heavy right eye and widened.

The shadow stepped between Kitty and the window, with the knife in its hand. I couldn't see the shadow's face, but I could see the vigorous movements of the right arm and shoulder up and down, back and forth, as it worked on Kitty Carlisle's once beautiful face with the knife. Her screams were deafening.

I felt a surge of panic and instantly hated myself for being afraid. I should have tried to save her, but right then chivalry was as dead as King Arthur.

I ducked down and made a fast break through the gap of trees and up the hill. When I got back to my car a quarter of a mile away, I could still hear Kitty's screams—or thought I could.

♣♣♣

I don't remember starting my car, but I was on the freeway before I even realized that I was driving, jamming hard on the gas back towards Potter's Marsh Road and forgetting there was a law called speeding.

Twenty minutes later I was home safe in my apartment, with a bad case of the heebie-jeebies.

I was out of my league. Whoever killed Kitty was certifiably psychopathic.

With a shaky hand I poured myself a drink and then poured another one. I should have poured the bottle down the sink, but I didn't. Instead I poured another one and another one, until the tip of my nose started to feel numb. Whoever named it whiskey got it all wrong. They should have named it *"More."*

I took the bottle into the bedroom. All I wanted to do was hide beneath the covers for a hundred years, but don't call me Elston Van Winkle, because an hour later I abruptly came awake to the sound of boots clacking on the back stairwell.

I bolted out of my bed and instinctively yanked my .38 out of its harness and pointed it at the door.

The clacking on the back stairs stopped.

I held the gun up to my eyes and broke the magazine out, ejecting the shell in the chamber. Then I put the magazine back, cocked it, and held the gun up, my finger on the trigger.

"I have a gun!" I called out.

The door suddenly swung open and a shadow stepped forward out of the darkness.

It was Melissa.

She was wearing the white raincoat with the hood thrown back. There were raindrops caught in her soft black hair, but the drops in her long eyelashes never came out of a Santa Rita sky.

Without warning she rushed into my arms. Something choked her in the throat, and her eyes grew hot with tears. Her back rocked with violent, shuddering sobs and the hot flush of tears burned on my bare chest.

I lifted her face off my chest and looked at her. Her right eye was badly swollen and discolored. Her bottom lip was split wide open. Her left cheek was bruised.

"Who did this to you?" I asked.

A strand of her hair hung down in a black fishhook over her forehead. I reached up and pushed the fishhook back in place, but it came right down again.

My lips were stretched across my mouth and I wanted to hurt something or tear somebody apart.

"What happened? Did *he* do this to you?"

She put both arms around my neck, tight, and slid her battered face against my neck.

"He went crazy." She was crying now in detached sobs, choking and gasping the words out. "He came home and started asking me all kinds of crazy questions. He called me a whore. He said I was nothing but a whore." Each sob was a ripping sound, as if it were torn out of her chest. "He hit me, Elston. He hit me and hit me and kept hitting me."

"Where is he now?" I asked.

"He left," she said, her lips held so tight that her teeth showed. "I think he went to the office. I think he was going to get his gun. The gun you told me about. That's all I kept thinking. He's going to get the gun and he's going to come back and kill me. I'm frightened, Elston. I'm scared to death."

I went to the kitchen and poured her a glass of whiskey. She took it and drank it as if the Four Horsemen of the Apocalypse had been sighted in Santa Barbara.

I brought her to the bedroom and made her lie down on the bed. Then I went to the closet and put my shoulder holster on, took the box from the closet shelf that held the extra shells, scooped up a handful of loose shells, dropped them in my pocket and left. I was out the door before I even knew I was moving.

Chapter Eighteen

Outside it was barely raining. It was more like the sky was spitting at me. I got in my heap and pointed it in the direction of Robert's office. The Santa Rita speed limit was twenty-five for business and residential areas. I hit sixty.

The rain was just getting heavy enough to reflect my headlights back at me. I flipped on the wipers. That made it worse, so I turned them back off. I could barely see the road in front of me. I almost went off into the gutters a few times. When I came to Sixth Avenue I slid the Electra to a bald-tire stop at the curb. No one was around. The street was deserted. The black bulk of Robert's office building squatted back from the pavement a half block away.

I sat there in my car for a few moments, wobbling a cigarette around and trying to make up my mind on how I was going to play this. I could hear the distant rumble of thunder over the hills and I timed my thoughts to its intensity.

I didn't know what I'd do when I found him in there. I imagined having Melissa all to myself, to never have to leave her, to come home to her every day and to keep her naked all night, but a confrontation with Robert didn't necessarily mean I would get what I wanted. I wouldn't be able to support Melissa the way she was used to being supported. But if a confrontation with her husband meant that we could be together, could I then force such a confrontation or allow one to happen?

I grabbed the flash out of the glove box, crossed the street, and went around to the mouth of the alley, taking in the black shadow of the building, the rain falling past the arc lights.

I threw my cigarette against the wall, and then I went down the side of the building into the darkness and slid the key Melissa had given me into the side door.

The door yawned back, stopped and began to swing forward again.

I slipped inside, closed the door softly and stood there for a moment, with my fingers resting on the knob. Nothing seemed out of place. All was darkness and shadows.

I turned on my flashlight and clawed my way down the long hallway, past Theresa Kramer's desk toward Robert's private office.

The door was almost insidiously ajar, a slice of soft yellow light shining through it.

I stood there for a moment and the hopelessness of the whole thing came heavy on me again.

I thrust my hat back and scratched under it, thinking, "What am I doing here? What do I expect to get from all this?"

I was taking too long to answer. This was one of those moments when you had to do it at white heat. Once you stopped and let yourself pussyfoot you couldn't go through with it any more.

I slid my .38 out of its sling, thumbed the hammer back and went into the room and looked at Robert Barrett.

He was sitting in the swivel chair behind the desk, with his back to me, in loose plum-colored pajamas and a Chinese coat.

A cigarette that he'd incompletely extinguished a few short moments ago was in a glass tray, stubbornly smoldering away. The drink that he'd started stood there on the edge of the desk. The white block of its still-unmelted ice cube peered through the side of the glass, through the straw-colored whiskey it floated in.

I leveled the .38 and walked slowly toward the desk.

"Mr. Barrett."

He didn't answer. This time I was a little louder.

"Mr. Barrett."

I expected him to be startled, but he didn't even flinch. The cigarette continued to unravel into smoke-skeins. The ice cube continued to peer through the highball glass, boxlike and unulcerated.

I went over to the side of the desk and almost slipped on his brains on the floor. I had to hold on to the corner of the desk to stop myself from falling into them.

The exit wound was dark and messy. There was dried blood hanging from the hair in front of his head, and a lacy cobweb pattern of black spread across the side of his face and across the hollow of his neck.

Robert Barrett was dead as a desert night and I knew there'd be hell to pay. You don't just squirt metal into someone as big as Robert Barrett and think you're going to get away with it. The buttons would be all over this like a hop-head on a stiff hooker of hooch.

I shined my flashlight against the wall. It was tinted an ugly blackish-red. There was a sliver of brain matter stuck on the wallpaper and the smell of death hung in the air, like raw meat before you put it on the grill.

I didn't know what to do.

Run?

Then what? Barrett was still dead. And I was the schmuck who was in love with his wife. The buttons would launch a full-scale investigation, and sooner or later it would lead them back to me. They'd find out somehow that I was having an affair with the corpse's wife.

Should I call the cops myself?

There would be lots of questions. Questions I didn't know how to answer. They'd put me under the lights, make me tell them what they wanted to hear. Why should they believe I had nothing to do with it?

And what about Kitty Carlisle getting her face sliced up like a Christmas turkey? How did that play into this whole mess?

Call the cops?

No thanks.

Should I make it look like it never happened? Make it look like Robert Barrett just dropped off from the face of the earth?

It would have to be a place where no one would remember having seen me or my car. Some quiet back road somewhere. It could be done. There would still be an investigation, but by the time it took the authorities to pin it on us, Melissa and I would be long gone.

Then I actually thought about it. It was crazy. This was murder. I was in over my head. It wasn't like the old days when someone shoved a retainer under Elston Brand's nose, held it out like a bone to a dog, asking him to tail a cheating husband or hush up a bit of extortion. This was *murder*.

I looked around the room.

The Bouguereau was hanging askew on the wall and the safe behind it had been emptied. The pictures on the desk had been thrown to the floor and the drawers were pulled out and scattered across the room.

The attaché case was gone. The money and drugs were gone.

Of course they were gone.

I stood frozen there, my head aching from thoughts that were too big for it.

The hole in Robert's temple was powder-burned and looked as if the shot came from a right angle. That meant whoever shot him was someone who could get in there and get close to him. I remembered the real pain in his eyes that first time when he told me he believed Melissa was having an affair. Now those eyes were lifeless and empty of all things. They had that effect the eyes of the new-dead have of almost, but not quite, looking at you.

His eyes seemed to be fixed on me, watching me, as if to say, "*What are you going to do now?*"

Those eyes seemed to follow me backward, step by step.

I went over a little to one side, and that didn't get me away from them. I went over a little to the other, and that didn't get me away from them either.

I could almost hear the droning words that went with those eyes: *"Where d'you think you're going now? What's your hurry? Come back here, Brand!"*

Suddenly, panic was licking all over me, like a shriveling, congealing, frigid flame.

Something moved behind the door.

A shuffle. A sound.

Then a disembodied hand reached for the light switch to the right of the doorjamb and the sudden illumination from the ceiling lights was like broken glass in my eyes.

Everything went dark for a quick second, and when it all came back into focus, I saw Frank standing in the doorway, and he had Updike with him.

"Drop the gun, Elston!" Frank said in a thick voice.

I looked down at the gun in my hand. Then I looked back up at Frank.

"I didn't do it, Frank. I didn't kill him."

Updike pointed his gat at me. "Drop that beanshooter, bo, or I squirt lead!"

I almost laughed. *Almost.*

"Drop the cannon, gumshoe!" Updike said again.

He was thoroughly enjoying this. I could tell by the look on his big ugly face. Yeah, he was enjoying this all right. He couldn't have been having a better time at a party.

I dropped my gun on the floor. Updike holstered his own piece and walked over to me, smiling like that damn Cheshire cat in *Alice in Wonderland.* Updike was one of those cops who loved to play god in this god-forsaken town.

"Remember me, tough guy," he said softly. "I'm your worst nightmare."

"I never forget a face," I said. "But in your case, I'll make an exception."

He threw me up against the wall, turned me around and frisked me. Then he took out his favorite pair of bone-pinchers and clamped them on my wrists.

"C'mon, Frank," I said. "Tell this gink to back off. You know I didn't kill anyone."

Frank shrugged. "You're here, ain't you, Elston?"

"Yeah, a little too conveniently," I said. "Who called copper, anyway?"

"Anonymous," Frank said.

"Figures."

He walked around the desk, took out a ballpoint pen, and picked up my gun with it.

"Check it," I said. "You'll see it hasn't been fired."

"Later."

He stuck it in his coat pocket.

"Hey, that's evidence," I said. "Aren't you supposed to handle it with kid gloves or something? I go to the movies, Frank. I know how it's supposed to be done."

"Close your head, Elston. I'll do the talking around here."

He went around the desk and squatted in front of what was left of Robert Barrett. Then he glanced down at the drawers strewn across the floor.

"Find what you were looking for, Elston?"

I stared at him expressionlessly.

Updike pulled roughly on the nippers and they dug deeply into the skin around my wrists. "Perhaps you don't hear so good, Shamus? The man asked you a question."

"Think about it, Einstein," I told him. "I fog Barrett for no reason and then wait around for you guys to show up? Someone set me up. Why don't you use your head, Nance?"

Updike slapped me on the side of the ear and my arms jerked so that I involuntarily cut my wrists on the handcuffs.

"You telegraph your punches," I told him. "You should stick to hitting people from behind. You're a thug with a badge, Up*tight*. A common masher. You're a disgrace to the police force."

He hit me again.

"Knock it off," Frank told him.

Updike looked at Frank with an almost hurt expression on his thick face, like a kid who's just been told to go to bed with no supper.

"You dumb mug," I said. "Get your mitts off the marbles before I stuff my foot down your mush."

Updike hit me a third time.

"I said knock it off!" Frank exploded.

"C'mon, Frank," I said. "You know I didn't kill Barrett. For once be a cop and not an ostrich. Take a whiff. Everything about this stinks."

"With the slime you associate with, Elston, I'm surprised you've still got a sense of smell. You've got nothing but larceny in you all the way from your balls to where you part your hair."

"Are you going to arrest me, Frank? Or just whisper sweet-nothings in my ear?"

"Yeah, I'm going to arrest you. But first I want to show you something."

♣♣♣

They left the handcuffs on as they dragged me out of Barrett's office and into the backseat of their unmarked car. Across the street I noticed that my Electra was already being towed and taken to impound.

"Where we going, Frank?" I asked from the backseat as Updike pulled out onto Sixth Avenue.

"Shut up," Frank said.

Updike turned left on Cajalco Road, past the Delaney Park Strip, and merged onto the freeway, heading south toward Deluge Point and Corona Del Mar State Park.

Then I knew where we were going.

We turned off at Potter's Marsh and continued west toward Turnagain Arm, through the winding roads and the still woods. A few minutes of that and we turned inland, into a hollow at the end of the gorge and then up on the high ground and down again and up again, until we got up to the ridge overlooking the silver-blue waters of Pescadero Bay and into the driveway of the small cottage.

We got out of the car and Frank steered me like a seeing-eye dog past the pile of cordwood and the double-bitted axe on a chopping block beside the front porch.

We ducked under the yellow police tape and walked into the cottage together and I was feeling like Jonah's ghost, as if I had just entered the belly of the whale itself.

Kitty Carlisle was sitting on the floor, her body rigid, her arms behind her, her head thrown back, her mouth open—like a patient in a dentist's chair. Half of her face was shining with blood where it had been worked on with the paring knife and her long tapered legs were coiled serpentine-like in the throes of death.

Two uniformed cops in wet, shining, rubber slickers were guarding the body like two-thirds of the three wise men standing over the manger. Frank dismissed them with a wave and popped a piece of Beech Nut chewing gum into his mouth.

"I believe you know Mrs. Carlisle," he said to me, snapping on his gum like a big turtle.

"She's looked better," I said.

If ever a face looked discolored and twisted and dead, it was the face of Kitty Carlisle. She looked as if she'd gone bad, as if she'd go all out of shape if you touched her. It was rigor mortis. It usually sets in after about three or four hours, but with the heat we'd been having it probably came on a lot quicker.

"I suppose you don't know anything about this?" Frank said.

I acted indignant, flattening my palm against my chest.

"Right," Frank shrugged, popping another piece of Beech Nut in his mouth. "You got an alibi for tonight?"

I should have told him everything I knew. After all, Frank and I went way back, but I didn't.

"I don't need an alibi, Frank. Lose the Sherlock Holmes act for a few minutes, will ya?"

Frank got a look on his face I'd never seen before. "Look at her, Elston! She's been sliced open like a fish."

I looked down at the former Kitty Carlisle aka Peaches. She hadn't died easily. The stark horror etched into the tight lines of her face showed that. Even in death, her eyes seemed to shine like uncut diamonds, grinning up at me with a cadaverous humor that seemed to blame me for not helping her when I had the chance.

I was starting to get angry. Angry at Frank for rousting me. Angry at Barrett for getting himself killed, and I was angry at myself for that moment of fear when Kitty was getting sliced up. I wrapped it all together in my gut and got it ready as a gift for whoever killed her.

"You gonna tell me how Robert Barrett ties into this whole thing, Elston?"

"I wish I could, Frank."

One of the M.E. guys came over and knelt down beside the body. He lifted one of Kitty's limp hands and stared at the fingernails.

"She's been dead about four or five hours," he said. "Better get her out of here, Frank, before she starts to get too stiff on us. We'll tell you the rest when we get her on a table."

"Go ahead," Frank said.

The M.E. nodded at his people and they zipped the body into its rubberized shroud, strapped the bag onto a stretcher and dragged away the pretty husk formerly known as Kitty Carlisle a.k.a. Peaches.

I turned away and Updike eagle-eyed me; running his tongue across his teeth, probing and flitting around for food particles or whatever treasures he might find in there.

"What do you want to do with this wise head, Frank?"

Frank looked at me and gleamed. "Book him. Stick him in a cell. Maybe then he'll think of something to tell us."

Chapter Nineteen

At precinct headquarters I was photographed, profile and full face. I was fingerprinted, stripped and given a cute little orange jumpsuit with LOS ANGELES COUNTY CORRECTIONS written on the back and a pair of matching skivvy slippers. The Santa Rita city lockup really knew how to treat its guests, and at the moment, I was the most distinguished guest on its list. I was the bird who clipped Robert Barrett, Attorney God of the Great Golden State.

After the initial processing, two burly guards led me down a long dimly-lit corridor. The skivvy slippers were too big for me and the only way I could keep them from falling off was to shuffle my feet without lifting them from the floor. But the guards didn't care; the slap-and-drag of my feet only annoyed them more. They just kept tugging at me and telling me to "C'mon! We ain't got all night, gumshoe!"

Finally we came to the end of the corridor and I was unceremoniously thrown into a cell. The walls were gray and filled with crude latrine drawings and ridiculous inscriptions: IF AT FIRST U DON'T SUCCEED, LOSING MAY JUST BE YOUR STYLE! BEAUTY IS ONLY A LIGHT SWITCH AWAY! DON'T TRUST ANYTHING THAT BLEEDS FOR 7 DAYS AND DOESN'T DIE! SCREW HOOVER HES GAY!

The high spot was a copulating pair made to look like a swastika.

It was loud and tight in there. And I wasn't alone. On one side of the room was a group of sulky-looking Mexican Zoot Suits and on the other, a gang of young black toughs; and stuck right smack in the middle of these friendly faces was yours truly, little old Elston Brand, private dick for hire. I thought about handing out my business card, but I had a feeling none of these gentlemen would be too interested in hiring me.

The two gangs were staring across the room at each other like two warring armies. And then, as sure as shit rolls downhill from a privy, one thing led to another, and all hell broke loose. Before you could even blink an eye, one of the black kids punched one of the Zoot Suits in the head, and sooner than later, there were bodies and fists flying everywhere.

I clenched my knuckles and got ready to start swinging at the first spic or smoke who came near me, when a hand fell on my shoulder and pulled me back.

I swung around and almost socked him in the pipes. He was a young black kid who would have been almost girlishly pretty if not for the look of defeat and oppression in his eyes. He was only seventeen or eighteen, but he looked like he had already seen enough violence and war to rival our boys across seas.

Before I could hit him, the kid held up his hands and nodded his head toward the door of the cell. A few seconds later the door flung open and a throng of bull guards came in, swinging their billy clubs all over the place, knocking everybody on the head and dragging them out of the cell for future tortures. After a few minutes of this, it was just me and the black kid all alone in the cell. He'd saved my skin and I hadn't even realized it.

Despite being a red-hot in one of Santa Rita's most notorious street gangs, the kid turned out to be an alright gee. I ended up spending the next twenty or so hours in that cell with him. For the first few hours he went on ranting and I got pretty tired of it pretty quick, but he was better than nobody to talk to.

"This your first offense, old man?" he asked me after a while, with a kind of hoarse softness, as if some cop had hit him across the windpipe with a blackjack once.

"First time I got caught," I answered him.

The kid seemed to be impressed by that. Eventually he fell asleep and then I had no one to kill time with except myself, and I've always felt that I'm pretty boring to talk to, so I laid there on my tiny cot and tried not thinking of anything.

It didn't work.

Melissa kept racing through my mind like a soft negligee on a hard woman, and thinking of her, away from me, was driving me crazy. She was underneath every word and every thought now. All I could think about was when I would get to see her again.

I closed my eyes and tried to sleep, but I couldn't.

There was no outside light, just the lambent electric bulbs shining in a silence that weighed several tons.

I laid there on the cold cot and listened to a guy in another cell singing *Molly Malone* in a whiskey tenor:

> In Dublin's fair city
> Where the girls are so pretty,
> I first set my eyes on sweet
> Molly Malone,
>
> As she wheeled her wheel-
> barrow, through streets broad
> and narrow,
> Crying "Cockles and mussels,
> alive, alive, oh!"
>
> "Alive, alive, oh,
> Alive, alive, oh,"
> Crying "Cockles and mussels,
> alive, alive, oh!"

It darkened early, that cell, earlier even then the grubby world outside. I thought about Melissa again. It's hard when you've got nothing to do but think. I thought of our short time together, in her bed, nipping at each other like puppies, and the last few days we spent together in my apartment, naked as two robins at a birdbath.

I thought about where she might be right now and what she might be doing. Did she know Robert was dead? Had she known he was dead all along? Did she know I had been arrested? Was she still at my apartment or had she gone back to her house?

Did I just happen to stumble into the wrong place at the wrong time when I went to Robert's office? Or did someone besides Melissa know I was going to be there?

I had a lot of unanswered questions that I wanted answered.

With no means to answer them I started silently swearing to myself until I ran out of four-letter words.

Then I started over again.

Chapter Twenty

A lot can happen to you in twenty hours. You begin to lose your sense of essentially. You stop telling yourself this sort of thing can't happen to you. It is happening to you, and you're afraid. It's a little trick the cops have to break you down. They sweat you out in a cell until you can't take it any longer, but I had something they couldn't sweat out, no matter how long they kept me in that cell. I graduated from Hard Knocks U, with honors, and I had the scars to prove it. I could take anything the coppers dished out. Underneath this wisecracking, hard drinking, chain smoking, tough exterior was a wisecracking, hard drinking, chain smoking, tough *interior*.

The morning crept in on all fours like a leper. My head ached, my back ached, and my legs throbbed. I tried to walk the stiffness off, but there wasn't much room in that steel box.

Someone brought me some cold coffee and a stale doughnut. Great. I sat on the edge of my cot and forced it down. At noon, I got a stale sandwich and warm milk.

After twenty hours I was starting to go batty; started seeing enormous sparrows and tiny Filipino prostitutes flitting about in the corner of my cell.

The cops can only hold you for twenty-four hours before they have to either charge you or release you. Like clockwork, on the twenty-second hour of my incarceration, the same two burly guards came into the cell and dragged me out. I got the distinct impression that they did not relish opening the steel doors nearly as much as they enjoyed closing them.

They led me down the long corridor of steel bars into another wing, passing through three sets of double doors, until we reached the gray hallway leading to an airless interrogation room called: "The Box."

The Box smelled like stale cigarette smoke, stale coffee and even staler bodily emissions. The burly guards threw me into a metal folding chair and told me to wait. The table and chairs were all screwed into the floor so you couldn't hit someone over the head with them. Just as I started wondering how long Frank was going to let me cool my heels in there, the hallway got noisy and I heard his cigarette-stained voice raising Cain with someone. Good old Frank.

The door slammed open and he stalked in, looking somber as ever. He was wearing a dark suit, properly rumpled, and a tie coming loose at the collar. Officer Updike accompanied him, and there was this gleam in Upt*ight's* eyes, as if he was getting a secret charge from all of this.

"Do you want a smoke?" Frank asked me.

"Sure," I said. "And how about a filet mignon?"

"Keep smiling, Elston," Frank said. "Whether you know it or not, you're in a heap of shit."

Frank poked a cigarette out from a full deck of Luckies and handed me one. His Borsalino hat was tilted back on his head. The shadows under his eyes were almost pits.

Updike leaned against the wall and tongued a cigarette from one side of his mouth to the other. This was Frank's show. Updike was just along for the ride, and the muscle, if need be. Maybe Frank thought if I clammed-up on him, I'd be more willing to give up the lay if my head was in a vice.

He opened a drawer in the table and pulled out a little notebook. Cops just love their little notebooks.

He dictated while he spoke aloud: "August 10, 1945, ten-ten p.m., interrogation by Lieutenant Merriwell of suspect in Robert Barrett murder investigation. What is your full name?"

"You talking to me, Frank?"

"Yeah, I'm talking to you, shithead. What is your full name?"

"Elston Millard Brand. But you can call me Shithead."

Frank didn't even crack a smile as he wrote in his little notebook. "Age and place of birth."

"Thirty-nine. Battle Creek, Michigan."

"Home address."

"You know where I live, Frank."

Suddenly Frank wasn't my friend anymore, if he ever had been. His eyes were too colorless and his face was too insipid and I was the guy under the lights who was going to answer his questions, and keep answering them until he was done with me.

"What is your home address, asshole?"

"41 West A Street. Santa Rita."

"Are you married? Have you even been married?"

"No. Yes."

"Parents living?"

"No."

"Do you have any criminal record?"

And on and on. Detective's dialogue. It comes out of an old shoebox. What they say doesn't mean anything, what they ask doesn't mean anything. It was rule one of interrogation. Not in the training manual, but written in stone. They just keep boring in until you are so exhausted that they hope you will screw up on some little detail.

Instinct, like an electrical wire running through me, jangled warningly: Make one admission, anywhere, along the line, and they'll have you, Elston, m'boy!

After several minutes of this, Frank stood up, sucked a long drag out of his cigarette and sat on the edge of the table, dangling his feet.

"Okay, now I'll get very simple in my questioning, Elston."

"Okay," I said.

"Why'd you do it?"

"Why'd I do what?"

"Why'd you kill Barrett?"

I laughed. There was nothing funny about it. "C'mon, Frank."

"Barrett was shot close up. Small-caliber gun, made a much bigger hole going out than going in. Brains splattered all over the place. Whoever did it got close to him. Barrett had his back turned. Takes a lot of courage to do that to a man." He interlocked his fingers and smiled at me, his eyes cold. "You use a small-caliber gun, don't ya, Elston?"

"Yeah, a .38 Special which you still have. You checked it yourself. You know it wasn't fired. In fact, Barrett had a .38 of his own. Whoever opened up his skull probably killed him with his own gun."

"Maybe you had another gun."

"You need to book a reservation on Realization Flight 110, Frank."

He swelled up like a toad. "Don't be a darb, Elston. This is the big time. A guy could get the electric cure for this."

"You've got nothing on me, Frank. There was no burn powder on me; my gun wasn't fired. Barrett was long dead before I ever went in there."

"Maybe you killed him earlier in the night, panicked, and went back to clean up the scene."

"You got the wrong guy, Frank, and you know it."

He distinguished his cigarette, which was threatening to torch his cuticles. "How can you sit there and lie like that, Elston, and look me in the face?"

"I'm getting used to your face."

"What, you think you got a fairy godmother or something?"

"No, but I've got an uncle I'm not sure about."

"They say that confession is good for the soul, Elston."

"Who's they?"

"I don't know. They. And they must mean it or they wouldn't say it. Got anything to confess, Elston?"

"Yeah, I stole an *Abba-Zaba* bar from Woolworth's when I was in the eighth grade."

Frank's boozy face was ready to split wide open. "You don't do well with authority, do you, Elston? Let me see, you never had a real job, am I right?"

"Yeah, you're right. I was a cop once."

Frank looked like he was trying to spit acid off the end of his tongue. "I could still bring you before the Magistrate and hold you for sixty days."

I reached for another butt and lit it. "Sixty days? I could do that standing on my head." I looked at Frank and smiled. "You're not trying to find a Chinese angle on this, are you, Frank?"

"We've got enough on you to send you to Folsom for a long time," he said, his voice raising an octave. "Now stop giving us the gooseberry and tell us what happened at Barrett's office."

"Don't I get a mouthpiece, Frank? Shouldn't I call my lawyer?"

"I haven't charged you with anything *yet*. I'm merely asking you a few questions. Besides, you don't have a lawyer. Who you kidding, Elston?"

"You're wrong, Frank. I've got a Jew lawyer named Abe Finklestien that'll have you reading parking meters."

He rubbed his jaw slowly. "What were you doing in Barrett's office?"

"I was working a case. Barrett was one of my clients. I needed to discuss something with him. The door to his office was open, so I went in. I found him lying there in his chair. That's when you guys showed up."

Frank pushed his lower lip out and let it snap back against his teeth. "What do you know about Barrett, Elston?"

"All I know is that he was a big-shot shyster and he had a lot of dough. He always had a bodyguard with him, some Roscoe named Dominick. I don't know his last name. Looked like he could've played football somewhere. Whoever chilled Barrett had to get around Dominick first."

"And where's this so-called Dominick now?"

"Probably in the unemployment line."

Even Updike couldn't help chuckling at that one. It was the first I'd heard from him in a while. Frank was the only one missing the joke.

"What about Kitty Carlisle?" he said, smoke drifting out of his nostrils. "Where does she fit into this whole thing?"

"Look, Frank, I don't know anything about Kitty Carlisle that you don't already know." I shrugged. "Barrett was knocking around with her on the side and she wound up dead. That's all I know."

Frank wasn't buying it. "We know someone hired you to follow Barrett, Elston. Who was it? Who hired you to follow Barrett?"

"I can't tell you that, Frank."

Frank laid it down, regarded me with a stare made out of acid. "Look, Elston, you can't play dumb on a murder case. Murder changes everything. I can hold you for contempt if you don't tell me who hired you and why."

Now that the chips were in the center of the table, I suddenly realized I was holding the wrong cards. I was holding a pair of deuces to Frank's full house and he knew it, and that's never a smart bet. A bluff now wouldn't last long.

I had to give him *something*. You got to have something to tell, that's it. You have to fill in all those places, and yet have it as near the truth as you can get it. But I wasn't about to tell Frank about Melissa or about the missing attaché case full of Florida snow. I know how cops in this town work. Even the best of them are a little crooked.

So I told him half of the truth; that I was working for Melissa. I wasn't too proud of myself for telling him even that.

Frank stood up and started pacing the room slowly. Then he stopped and stood there at the table looking down at me with a cold light in his eyes.

"Why did Melissa Barrett hire you?"

"She thought Barrett was going to kill her."

"Did she ever appear to be abused?"

"*Abused?*"

"Beat up. Any black eyes or split lips?"

"Yeah. One time."

"When was that?"

"Last night."

"Last night? The same night her husband was killed and you were found at the murder site?"

"That's right, Frank. She came to see me. She said Barrett hit her and that he threatened to kill her."

"Then you went to his office to find him?" Frank said, his voice hard and gravelly; as if a bullet were caught in his throat. "Sir Galahad to the rescue, is that it, Elston?"

I was feeling tired, used up, drawn out and sapped. My throat was sore from smoking and yapping so much and my brain ached from trying to keep all my thoughts in line.

Frank leaned over the table, his hands on the edge for support, staring down at me like I was a piece of meat in a butcher shop window.

There were tiny lights in his eyes, gray as .30-30 bullets. "Well, smartguy, did you know that Melissa Barrett is missing? Did you know that?"

I grimaced and made a disgusted sound, as though I'd just tasted something rotten.

"Yeah, that's right, Romeo," Frank said, a slick greasy smile on his face. "It just happens that a large sum of money was withdrawn from Barrett's savings account on the afternoon he was murdered. Ten large to be exact."

Suddenly the whole damn calliope came crashing to the ground and the steam organ started playing "Taps" in my head.

I tried to swallow but my Adam's apple got stuck in my throat. I think I must have looked as sick as I felt.

Frank kept spitting the words out between his teeth: "We think pretty little Melissa Barrett lammed off with the money and got *you* ribbed to take the fall." His voice was prodding me now like a gun barrel, hoping for any kind of a slip-up. "Melissa Barrett sizes up as a worker, Elston; a woman who kills her husband for his money and leaves a sap like you to do the dance."

He had me in his crosshairs now. It was one false move, and baby the lights go out.

"Is that how it went down, Elston? Did Melissa Barrett tell you she loved you? I'll bet she made you feel like a man again, didn't she? It was easy for her. She smoked her husband and scrammed out with his scratch and made a clean sneak of it. She just needed a rube to cool, and you were that rube, weren't you, Elston? When she first came around, didn't it ever even occur to you, the whole thing? After all, what would a dame like Melissa Barrett see in a loser like you? A babe like that plays ball in a bigger league than you can pay admission to see. It didn't seem a little prearranged to you, Elston?"

Let him beat my heart out, I thought dismally. Let him beat me up to his heart's content. I wasn't going to let him flimflam me into spilling my guts all over the floor.

"C'mon, Elston. Put us wise. Be a wise head and tell us where she is."

"I don't know where she is."

And that was the truth. I wanted to know where she was far worse than he did.

I groaned inwardly as the truth slithered out in the open and stared me in the face. *Could she have done it?* Could she have killed Robert and lammed-out with his dough, leaving me to fry the bacon? Could she have double-crossed me like that? I'd seen enough high heels and raw deals, enough single malts and double crosses in my lifetime to know that she could have, but hell, that couldn't be right. It...

Frank laughed; a tight sneering little laugh. "You're a fool, Elston. Barrett carried more insurance than Prudential. Melissa figures to collect another three-hundred g's if you go down for her husband's murder."

He wanted some reaction out of me, but I wasn't going to give it to him. I was too damn tired.

I tilted my head sideways and looked up at him. "Are you charging me now, Frank? Because if not, then you have to let me go. I know my rights. You can't hold me here for more than twenty-four hours, and it's now..." I looked at the clock on the wall behind him very slowly for effect. "Twenty-three hours and fifty-four seconds, to be exact."

Frank looked at me for what seemed a long time. The tension slowly siphoned from the room and left a sort of vacuum behind it. Then he threw a backhand wave at me.

"You're free to go, Elston." I'd got myself a stay, but not yet an acquittal: "Just don't go take yourself a notion to disappear like your girlfriend did. I want you where I can find you. You leave the city limits and I'll haul your ass back in here and lock you up for good as a material witness. Savvy?"

Chapter Twenty-one

I was escorted into a small cubicle for out-processing where a bald middle-aged police clerk with three chins and a bad case of hemorrhoids checked off my personal belongings against a list made when I was first picked up. Like a tired auctioneer, he recited a brief description of each item:

"One inexpensive wristwatch, one pack of Dubble Bubble chewing gum, one lottery ticket, one unused prophylactic, one half-empty pack of Lucky Strike cigarettes, two silver or gold-plated finger rings, one black Brooks Brothers suit jacket, one robin's-egg-blue tie with a touch of real egg still on it, one pair black suit pants, one white Arrow shirt, one beige Borselino hat with black leather band. Two dollars and eighty-four cents. Sign the receipt."

He handed me a pen and I made an X at the bottom of the form. They wouldn't give me back my gun. State's evidence, they called it.

"I hope you found our accommodations to your liking," the clerk said with a well-practiced cynicism.

"Terrific," I said. "Just terrific."

Ten minutes later I passed the main sally port and went down to the impound lot to retrieve my car. The twenty-five bucks it cost me to get it back was just insult to injury. It was legalized extortion. Thank you, Santa Rita P.D.

I got in and pushed the Electra back into the flattening heat of Cahuenga. The streets had that tired gray look which is a combination of too late at night and too early in the morning.

I turned on Canal Street and parked in front of the Red Carpet. Angie was behind the bar, smoking and listening to the jukebox pouring out its breathless, slippery jazz.

The place was nearly empty and when Angie saw me she looked like I was the cow that kicked over the lamppost.

"Jesus, Elston, what happened to you now? You look like you haven't slept in a month."

I took off my hat and sat down at the bar. "Funny thing happened," I told her, and told her about the funny thing. "I spent last night playing button-button with the cops down at the Crowbar Hotel. I got the hammer and saw on me for a murder I didn't do."

"It's that Barrett guy, ain't it?"

"Yeah. How'd you know?"

"It was all over the evening rags."

"Someone used the back of his head for target practice," I told her.

"And the cops think you killed him?" she asked, her voice fluttering like a kite. "You didn't...did you?"

I looked up at her. "C'mon, Ang."

"Sorry."

"Accepted."

I flipped a butt into my mouth and gave the rest of the story to her in short order.

She chewed her lower lip and thought it over. "That tomato you were in here with the other night; that was Barrett's wife, wasn't it?"

"Uh-huh. And the cops think she bumped him off and got me to help."

"I hate to say this, Elston, but I ..."

I flapped my paw. "Yeah, yeah, I know. You told me so."

I caught my reflection in the mirror behind the bar and stared at it. I wondered if I was as ugly to others as I was to myself. And what was on the outside was no comparison to the way I felt on the inside.

"I've been down and I've been out," I whined to my favorite bartendress. "I've been busted, dusted, crusted and disgusted. I've gotten sunstroke, frostbite, poison ivy, Rocky Mountain Fever and the blind staggers, but I've never been this down before, Ang. I don't know if I'm coming or if I'm going anymore."

Angie wasn't about to give me any sympathy. "Yeah, well get used to it, buddy. Look at me. I slop barley twelve hours a day in this dive, but I ain't got no regrets. The day you start regretting, well, then you've already given up the game. I am who I am, and I'm not going to regret anything."

Right then she was the most beautiful woman in the world and I started asking myself questions why we never made it full-time. Maybe we were too much alike. I don't know.

I finished my beer and got up. Angie looked at me sadly and leaned over the bar and kissed me on the lips.

"What was that for?" I asked.

She smiled a smile that was as fragile as Dresden china.

"For old times' sake."

Chapter Twenty-two

I got back in the Electra and drove through the neon industrial dawn to my apartment. It had been a long couple of nights and I was dog-tired. All I wanted to do was crawl out of my dirty clothes like a snake and go to sleep. Then I decided that there was probably no point in going to sleep, since that's exactly what I had been throughout this whole thing—asleep.

I parked the Electra in the alley and climbed the back stairs and used the bar-lock door to get in. The place was dark and musty, like any place that has been locked up for a few days. It made me feel like an embalmed corpse just being back there.

I flipped on the light and that's when someone hit me behind the ear, flush on the mastoid bone, and a pool of darkness opened up at my feet, draining the starch from my legs.

I shook off the blow and got a leg bent and a knee under me. Then I came up grunting hard and climbed the rest of the way, the taste of blood in my mouth, swaying a little, prowling the room with my eyes.

Jimmy the Weasel was standing there, smiling like the stupid Dago that he was.

I made a fist and hit him on the chin. All I did was hurt my hand.

Jimmy smiled again and then hit me with a fist as big as a trailer tractor bumper.

There was a blinding flash inside my brain and fireworks behind my eyes and I went down like a poled steer.

"He won't kill you, Elston..." a disembodied voice said from some far corner of the room. "Unless I tell him to."

The voice brought me up from some darker pit than sleep. I looked around and saw Bedbug Santucci sitting in my favorite uneasy chair by the window.

"Get out of my chair," I said.

He showed me some of his gold teeth when he smiled. I was getting damn sick of those gold teeth. Pretty soon I'd be seeing those gold teeth in my dreams and I didn't like it. When I dream I prefer pink elephants and fuzzy puppies.

Bedbug stood up from the chair and I took the opportunity to rush him, but Leadpipe Moceli came out of the shadows and put me in a full-nelson. I should have known better. Whenever Jimmy the Weasel was around, Leadpipe was never far behind.

It was hard to talk with Leadpipe's arms around my throat, but I managed to say, "I already paid you, Bedbug."

"Not all of it, Elston," Bedbug said. "You only paid me a grand. The debt was twelve hundred. With interest, I'd say you still owe me five bills. But I didn't come here to personally collect on that small change."

"What the hell did you come here for then?"

With a nod of Bedbug's head, Leadpipe released me from the stranglehold he had me in.

I pulled up and straightened out my wrinkled suit. My throat felt as though it had been through a mangle.

"Shall we have a drink, Elston?" Bedbug said, strolling over to the kitchen table. "By the way, your style in home décor is quite *quaint*."

"Just tell me what you want and get the hell out."

He shrugged his shoulders, which were adorned in a natty three-piece dark blue suit with white pinstripes and a little blue handkerchief peeking out of the left breast pocket. His tanned face looked shadowy above the dark colors.

"I've been partaking in your fine choice of whiskey while you were out," he said, picking up the bottle of Seagram's and pouring himself a good stiff one into a chunky glass. "Care to join me?"

"Go to hell," I said. "And take your monkeys with you."

He picked up the glass of whiskey and finished it off with one loud gulp. "Not bad. It ain't Chivas, but it's not bad. When I was a kid we used to drink Mad Dog 20/20. Cheap shit; but it did the job. Now I can afford the crème de la crème. Five-Star Martell if I want it."

"Fascinating," I said. "But you didn't come all the way over here to discuss the merits of my whiskey. If it's the five hundred bucks you want…"

"I told you I didn't come here to make a personal house call on what you owe me, Elston." He poured himself another shot of whiskey and strolled around the kitchen table and sat down in my easy chair again. He folded one leg over the other, and said, "Word on the street is that Kitty Carlisle met a rather unpleasant fate."

"Word on the street travels fast," I said, rustling a cigarette out of my suit pocket and flopping it in my mouth. "Did you kill her?"

"You amuse me, Elston."

"I'm glad I amuse you. But you didn't answer the question. Did you kill Kitty?"

"Don't be a frube, Elston," he said, touching the ends of his little moustache with two fingers, the nails of which had a purplish tint. "You ain't talkin' to some dago just off the boat. I run a legitimate business. I've never claimed to be an advertisement for the Better Business Bureau, but I'm not stupid either. A dead hooker who worked in my establishment would have to point to me. I'd be fingering myself. I have no idea why someone would want to kill Kitty. She was a nice piece of ass, but no single piece is worth killing for."

"Maybe Kitty wanted out of the business. Maybe she wanted out, and you *terminated* her employment. Maybe you killed her and her rich boyfriend the alderman and expected his wife to take the fall."

He just sat there, unflinching and as cool as snowmelt. "If Kitty wanted out, she could have gotten out. All she had to do was ask, and I'd let her walk. But she didn't want out. She loved the juice."

"You would have let her walk? Just like that?"

"Just like that," he said, snapping his fingers.

"So why break into my place and tell me about it?"

"I want you to do something about it."

I dragged on my butt and blew a cloud of smoke in his face. "What do you want me to do about it?"

"Find out who killed Kitty, before the buttons try to pin it on me."

"You've got a syndicate. *You* find out who did it."

He made a vague motion with his head and Jimmy and Leadpipe hit me in the stomach simultaneously. I could feel the blood rising between my chest like heartburn and the air in my lungs was so hot it choked me.

Bedbug shrugged, as if it were a matter of no consequence. "Syndicate is a word I don't like to use," he said, his eyes glowering at me with dislike and distaste. "When I hear that word I think of comic strips and advice-to-the-lovelorn columnists like Dorothy Dix. The people who distribute that crap to newspapers are syndicates. The organization I work for has nothing to do with cartoons or advice-to-the-lovelorn. I'm not gonna let the buttons put this thing on me and disrupt my *organization*. You came around my place asking about Kitty, so that makes me think you know something."

I told Bedbug I didn't know anything about Kitty's murder.

He nodded and Jimmy and Leadpipe slugged me again. This time I was barely able to keep the blood and bile from my gut exploding out of my mouth like a volcano.

Despite the pain I smiled, and then allowed the smile to become a laugh. People should laugh, don't you think? There's too much seriousness in the world.

"You're not God," I said, spitting out some of my blood on Bedbug's natty suit. "You're not even Jesus Christ."

He took out the little handkerchief from his breast pocket, dabbed at my blood on his suit, refolded the handkerchief carefully, and put it back in his breast pocket.

His eyes measured me for a coffin. I wasn't scared. I was paralyzed.

"I want you to find out who killed Kitty. You do this for me, Elston, and we're even."

The way I saw it I had no choice. Refuse and Bedbug would fit me for cement shoes.

"Okay," I said. "I'll do it. But I need some information first."

Bedbug shrugged. "Name it, partner."

"I need to know if there's been any unusually large shipments of heroin out on the streets."

He looked confused. "There was a big score last week. No one knows where it came from."

"How big was the score?" I asked.

"Huge."

"How huge is huge?"

"Quarter of a mill huge. The market's all closed-up now. Nobody can move anything. What's all this got to do with Kitty's murder?"

I stroked my mouth as though the words tasted rotten even before they'd come out. "That's what I'm going to find out for you," I said.

He held out his hand and I shook it.

Me and Bedbug Santucci. Partners in crime. A couple of real pals. Two smart boys side by side. Santucci and Brand. Brand and Santucci. Had a nice ring to it. Made me want to wretch.

There wasn't much else to say. There wasn't much else said. When Bedbug and his supergoons left I got up and poured the rest of Bedbug's drink down the sink and rinsed the glass. Then I turned back my cuffs and splashed cold water on my face and toweled dry. I felt like something that had washed up on the beach.

I went into the bedroom, shut the window against the morning heat, and then there was nothing left to do but think about all the things I couldn't prove until I fell asleep. Which I did.

♣♣♣

The dream was clear as daylight:

Melissa was on the shore of a beach, the waves from the ocean lapping at her pretty pink toes. I went to her but she kept getting farther and farther away. She was smiling at me in the sun, urging me to follow her, but I couldn't get to her. It was as if my feet were stuck in quicksand. I looked over my shoulder and saw Barrett riding on my back, his legs clamped around my waist, his arms around my throat; blood pouring down his face, and he was laughing at me like a freak in a carnival side show...

Chapter Twenty-three

I woke up feeling like I hadn't slept. Then came noon, and morning withered like a lost dream. When the sun got hot enough it burned away all the illusions and I saw Santa Rita for what it really was—cheap, surly, and insolent—nothing good ever happened here.

I went to the kitchen, threw some aspirin down my throat and went downstairs to the little newspaper vendor on the street. Barrett's kill was spread all over the afternoon edition of the sheets.

I took the paper with me up to my apartment and shook it out.

It was there, all right. Page one. Right next to the announcement that the Japs were willing to surrender provided that Emperor Hirohito remained in power.

Murder is always good copy, particularly when it happens to the rich and regal. Robert Barrett had been both, and for the next few days all the insalubrious details of Barrett's life would be covered with apt relish by all the ragpushers along the

West Coast until another lurid story reared its ugly head.

I put the paper down and tried to get focused. I needed to find Melissa, but I didn't even know where to start. I was banging my head against a stone wall, and I didn't like the feeling.

The cops thought Melissa killed Robert and that I helped her do it, but they wouldn't have let me loose if they had any positive proof. They were either hoping I'd turn up something on my own, or they were hoping I'd betray myself or Melissa.

In any case, I had a lot to do to clear my name and there was no telling how much time I had before Frank put the charge on me.

Out of desperation I picked up the phone and had the operator put me through to the only friend I had left on the Santa Rita police force. Someone at precinct headquarters put the call through and Evinrude Neptune Johnson barked a hello into the phone.

"Hey, Rudy, it's Elston."

"Oh, God," he exclaimed.

"Just Elston is fine."

"What trouble have you gotten yourself in now?"

"What makes you say that?"

"Because Elston Brand wears trouble like a king wears a crown. And whenever Elston Brand's in trouble, he calls Rudy."

Rudy Johnson was a fifteen-year veteran of the Santa Rita Police Department, but the higher-ups stuck him behind a desk because he was a big Negro who didn't know his place. Rudy wasn't afraid of the brass and he spoke his mind whenever he felt it was necessary. Once, when a captain from the Fifth Precinct called him a spearchucker, Rudy broke the guy's nose. The department would have simply swept the incident under the carpet if Rudy would have apologized to the captain, but he wouldn't, so he was forever banished to a life of cubicle slavedom, pushing papers and typing traffic violation reports. Police Purgatory.

Rudy owed me a couple of favors and I was collecting one now:

"What do you know about Robert Barrett?" I asked.

"I know he's dead."

"Barrett was a client of mine," I said. "*Was* being the hundred-dollar word. Homicide thinks I did it."

"Who put you in The Box?" Rudy asked.

"Frank," I said.

"Merriwell's alright. He's one of the few peepers in this department you can actually trust."

"Yeah, I used to think so, too. But Frank tried to put the screws on me."

"But he let you go?"

"Had to," I said. "No gun. My .38 wasn't fired and there were no powder nitrates on me. Frank kept me in the cooler for the full twenty-four. He was trying to sweat me out. Then he stuck me in The Box with a bull who would love to get his mitts on me."

"Who's the bull?"

"Goes by the name Updike."

Rudy exhaled into the receiver. "Updike used to box professionally before he became a cop. All the sleuths on homicide use him for muscle. I wouldn't mess with Updike, Elston."

"I've dealt with bigger palookas," I said, trying to sound tough, but I doubt that it was working.

"There's something you're not telling me, Elston," Rudy said. "Something doesn't add up. Why did Robert Barrett hire you?"

"To look after his wife. He was convinced she was cheating on him."

Rudy sighed enormously, a man of immense telephonic gestures. "You didn't get up close and personal with the Alderman's wife, did you, Elston? Guys have been sliced up and thrown in the Santa Rita Harbor for looking at Barrett's wife. I met her a couple of times at police functions. Christmas parties and what not. She's a real dish. You're gonna wind up getting yourself killed, racing around the track with that little filly. Besides, that's just bad business. Sleeping with the wife of a client. Even for a low-down eye like you, that's just bad business."

"Calm down, Sherlock," I said. "She was a client of mine before he was."

Rudy took another minute to digest that one. "I don't understand. You were working for both of them?"

"That's right."

"Ain't that a conflict of interest, Elston? Or don't you private guys subscribe to that moral code?"

"Morals don't mean much in my line of work, Rudy."

"I suppose you hit the nail on the head with that one. What did Barrett's wife hire you for?"

"She thought Barrett was going to kill her."

"The plot thickens, eh? Where's she at now?"

"Nobody knows. Frank thinks she split town with Barrett's money and a stash of H he had hidden in his office."

"What do you think happened to her?"

"I don't know what I think, Rudy. I don't know anything anymore. But I have to find out. She's the only alibi I've got. If I don't, then I'm a dead pigeon. The heat is on and the fire is burning a lot of people in this city. I heard the mayor himself is changing his pants hourly while the investigation is ongoing. What have you heard about Barrett's girlfriend? She was killed up in Potter's Marsh."

"Barrett had a stable of girls."

"This one was special. Blonde, tall. Someone did some knife work on her."

"I heard about it," Rudy said. "But that's all. There's a wall around it. I've been iced out. Homicide's keeping everything to themselves. Frank's got unis at Barrett's office twenty-four hours a day. Apparently Barrett had a secretary that Frank wants to get his mitts on."

"Theresa Kramer," I said.

"What?" Rudy asked.

"The secretary's name is Theresa Kramer."

"Well, my friend," Rudy said. "I'd suggest you talk to this Theresa Kramer before Frank does."

Chapter Twenty-four

Back out on the street, the heat hit me like a wet dishtowel. I got in the Electra and headed it toward Barrett's office. Circling through the tight streets, I backtracked several times, making sure no elbows were tagging me.

When I hit Juniper I turned the corner and parked down the block where I still had a clear view of Barrett's office. The cops were planted all over the place.

I sat there with all the windows rolled down to alleviate the heat and waited. About an hour later a fresh-faced cop in a blue uni came out the front door with a woman at his side. She wore her pale blonde hair short in the Italian style with Medusa tendrils giving it a Bohemian, uncombed effect. She was wearing a skirt and sweater with a short coat thrown over her shoulders and she looked like a teenager out on a date.

Theresa Kramer smiled demurely up at the uni and he smiled back at her. I had a feeling she could deck a man with that smile.

She got in a little convertible sedan and drove off, and the uni stood there like a pimply-faced sophomore who has been left high and dry on Prom day.

I followed Theresa Kramer's convertible sedan. She had an attendant gas her up at a Sinclair station on Pico Avenue, then she drove up into the mountains.

She had a nice little place on Mount Curve Boulevard. Nothing fancy. Just a simple one bedroom bungalow surrounded by carefully trimmed shrubbery and a lawn as smooth as a putting green. It was as homey as a Norman Rockwell cover.

She parked the sedan in the driveway and went inside the house. I parked on the other side of the street, got out and went up the veranda to the front door. I knocked twice before I heard a muffled sound from inside.

"Coming!"

She answered the door and her smile was as good as the sun. She was a natural blonde with a healthy complexion and very little make-up. She stood straight and was full of bouncing energy.

"Yes? May I help you?"

In my best cop voice, I said, "My name's Merriwell." Hell, Frank wouldn't mind if I borrowed him for a few minutes. "I work for the Santa Rita Police Department. May I come in, Mrs. Kramer? I'd like to ask you a few questions about your employer, Robert Barrett."

"You're investigating Robert's murder?"

"More or less."

Her eyebrows pulled together slightly. "I just got done talking to the cops back at the office."

"Yes, that's right, but I'm the lead detective on the case. I just missed you at the office. I'd like to go over everything personally instead of reading it from the reports. You understand, don't you, Mrs. Kramer?"

Something went tight and strange in the look she gave me. She pulled the sleeves of her white sweater down over her hands, balled the ends up in her palms, leaned on one leg.

At first I didn't think she was going to let me in, but then the look was gone and she had the door unhooked and she asked me to come in.

The room was simple and well kept: a chesterfield and matching armchair, a coffee-table, a portable record player on a stand with a pile of Frankie Lane records beside it, a magazine rack containing a *Cosmopolitan,* a couple of copies of *Mademoiselle,* and a cheap reprint of a historical romance.

There were no pictures on the wall, and no photographs anywhere. Either she hadn't lived there long, or she didn't plan on staying. Even a migratory bird leaves more permanent traces than she had.

A cardboard box containing her personal belongings from work was on the floor in the middle of the room.

"I have to find a new job," she said, nodding her head at the box.

I immediately liked her voice. Kind of smoky like Jean Harlow, but friendly, too, like Carol Lombard.

She took out a deck of cigarettes and sat down in the chesterfield.

"You don't mind if I smoke, do you?" Then, with a little nervous laugh, she said, "What am I saying? This is my house, I can smoke if I want to."

When she was finished lighting a long cigarette, she blew the match out. "I just put on some water for tea. Will you have some?"

"No thank you," I said. "I don't drink anything lighter than beer."

"I thought cops couldn't drink on duty?"

"That's an old wives' tale." I lit a cancer stick of my own and sat down in the armchair. "I'm sorry you lost your job."

She was perched on the couch like a bird waiting for a signal to take flight. "Life goes on," she said, letting the smoke filter through her lips.

"Not for Mr. Barrett it doesn't."

She lengthened her mouth at the corners in an expression of dull irony. On the stove, the teapot had just begun to simmer.

"No, I suppose it doesn't," she said, her white hands wrestling each other in her lap. "What's a job compared to being murdered, right?"

"Nicely put," I said, with a touch of dull irony of my own. "What was he like?"

"Who?"

"Your boss. Robert Barrett."

"Of course. How silly of me." She moved her hand over her mouth and puffed on the cigarette. "He was strict, but fair. Robert was always fair. Hey, you got a badge?"

I nodded. "I got a badge. Want to see it?"

She waved her hand in front of her face as though she were brushing away a spider-web. "Forget it. It's just that you hear about fake cops trying to get into a girl's home and..."

She was a dame who read too many dime-store novels.

"I'm as real as it gets," I told her.

The teapot grew shrill.

"Excuse me," she said.

She went into the kitchen and a few seconds later emerged with a cup of something that looked like ditchwater.

"Sure you don't want some?" she asked, blowing steam off the top of the cup. "It's Dai Pai Dong."

"I'm sure it is," I said. "Sounds tasty, but no thanks."

She took a sip and watched me with her eyes peering over the rim of the cup.

"What'd you say your name was again?"

"Merriwell. Frank Merriwell."

She set the cup down and picked up her cigarette again. "I'm afraid I don't know anything about Robert's murder, Detective Merriwell."

I kept my voice low and friendly, pleasant, and as cop-like as possible. "What about his habits?"

"What about them?"

"Well, did you notice anything unusual about Robert's activities lately?"

"No," she said, snapping cigarette ashes at me with her thumbnail. "Nothing unusual that I can think of."

She spoke monotonously, as if she had said the same thing several times already.

"Did any of Robert's friends ever drop by the office?"

"No. Nobody except..."

"Except...?"

She shook her head. "No one."

"How about Mrs. Barrett? Did she ever come to the office?"

"Melissa? No, she never came to Robert's office. In the three years that I worked for Robert, I never saw Melissa at the office."

"But you knew her?"

"Of course. We used to see each other at work parties and other functions sometimes. I liked her a lot. But I always felt sorry for her in some way."

"Why's that?"

Theresa Kramer brought her cigarette to her lips and allowed the smoke to waft over her face, like a veil.

"Robert was cheating on her, Mr. Merriwell." A look of real pain touched her face. "I hated it, but I couldn't say anything to Melissa. It would mean my job. I had to pretend I didn't know anything."

"Who was the other woman?" I asked.

"I don't know. I never asked." Her eyes went narrow and her voice barb-wired. "But Melissa got back at him."

"What's that?"

"I said Melissa got back at Robert for his infidelity."

There was a catch in my voice, the briefest stutter. "How did she manage that?"

"She started seeing someone."

"Who?" I asked. It came out of me like an owl on barbiturates.

A smile moved almost imperceptibly from her eyes to her mouth, but didn't stay.

"She never told me a name, but she did tell me she was in love. She deserved that, you know? Love. Everyone deserves love."

"When did Melissa tell you this?"

"We were at the club. Robert was throwing a birthday party for her. Melissa had a few drinks and it just sort of slipped out when we were alone. You know, girl talk."

"The club?" I asked.

"The Barrett's belong to the Mariposa Canyon Golf Club. Real swanky place. I heard you have to have a million dollars just to work in the bar."

"Is that the one Ben Hogan built out on Earthquake Park?"

Her voice was neutral, but under the neutrality lay the zest of an innocent bystander waiting to see the first blood in a barroom debate. "That's the one."

Chapter Twenty-five

The Mariposa Canyon Gulf Club was as pretentious as its name, with solid glass doors, timber siding, big glass windows and a smell of real money. A couple tons of shiny Cadillac, Jaguar, and Lincoln were parked in the parking lot.

I felt out of place as I eased the Electra past well-tanned men and women on their way to the clubhouse. Everything looked clean and prosperous, except me.

Walking through the solid glass doors I went over to the front desk clerk, the one with the dreary sneer. He was a tall, lanky little pantywaist with an egg-shaped head, a pencil-thin moustache, and a wrist so limp it was virtually held together by elastic.

"This is a private club," Pantywaist said. With a full day's growth of beard and the wrinkled ruin of a suit I had on, I was lower than the janitor in his estimation.

"I thought maybe I could join your club," I said.

He snickered and gave me an expression like I spat on windshields. With an air of practiced cordially, he said, "Maybe you can and maybe you can't. Write us a letter and we'll let you know."

Snobbery and fastidiousness were not simply character traits with this gaycat; they were flags that he flaunted with pride.

"May I at least have a word with the manager?" I said.

He shook his pretty little head. "No, no, no. Absolutely not."

I heard music and noticed a lot of people coming out of a ballroom off to one side. Some kind of party was going on. I turned my head to get a better look, but Pantywaist got in my way. His thin eyebrows shot up and his mouth puckered.

"I think you ought to leave now, sir."

His voice set my teeth on edge. For the last week I'd been pushed around and knocked down and I was in no mood to take it now from a little gaycat in a three-piece suit. My back was against the wall and my fangs were just starting to come out.

I reached around and harvested a fistful of the lapels of his fancy suit.

"Look here, Nancy," I said, thrusting my kisser two inches from his, so he could smell the blood in my breath. "I'm about this close from sticking my foot up your ass and making you the first human Popsicle. By the way you look, you might think you'd enjoy it, but you won't."

"Let go of me!" he squawked, flapping like a hen laying a square egg.

Pantywaist's face went all white as he fell back to earth in a puddle of his own pretension, but then his eyeballs ballooned as he caught sight of something or someone behind me.

I smelled the guy behind me—he smelled faintly of Middle Eastern cigarettes—but before I could even drop Pantywaist, he sapped me hard behind the ear with a leather blackjack. You could hear the plunk above the music from the ballroom. It sounded exactly like somebody thumping their finger against a watermelon.

I stood there, an idiotic grin on my face, and then I got hit again.

I wobbled on my legs and then I went down, the world rushing away from me and I found myself dropping down a long, narrow tunnel that ended when the floor jumped up and slapped me in the face.

♣♣♣

I was too numb to feel much pain, but the carpet under my face was wet and in need of a haircut. I thought I tasted the wool and dust. I was barely conscious. Someone nearby groaned. It was a familiar voice, yet far away, like a voice on a radio on the other side of a street, and after a while I recognized it as my own.

I sat up, a hammer of pain beating at the base of my skull. At first all I could see was a tiny circle of light, like a circle of wet, yellow paper. Then the blackness lifted and the circle got bigger and bigger.

I was lying on a floor, sniffing the dust off the hairy carpet, in a room that could have been a broom closet. There was a scarred, green metal desk with a chair behind it, a bulletin board, and a filing cabinet. There was a picture of Ben Hogan on one wall and a picture of General George Patton on the other. The entire room conflicted with the luxurious elegance of the golf club, and yet a subconscious feeling existed that I was still within the club's wealthy confines.

The guy who sapped me was sitting behind the desk. He was a thickset blob with enormous black worms for eyebrows and absolutely no hair on his head. A well-built Sydney Greenstreet look-alike. The smoke from his Turkish cigarettes was making me nauseous.

I rubbed the back of my head where he had hit me. Everything was a blur coated in pain. There was a big welt behind my ear and it hurt like eight bitches in a bitch boat just to touch it.

"Why'd you dry-gulch me?" I asked Mister Greenstreet.

He brought the long Turkish cigarette away from his lips, tilting his head back so that the smoke didn't get in his eyes.

"You were being quite unruly out there, Mr. Brand," he said, in a voice too comfortable with command. "I felt it was necessary to give you a little..." Here he giggled like a little girl with a secret... "*sap poison.*"

He seemed like he took great pleasure out of giving me a little sap poison. I started wondering how the hell he knew my name, and then I saw my wallet laid out on his desk, along with the sap he had used to brain me. It was a black woven thing with a coil spring handle. It looked like something you might find in a kinky Filipino bar, if you're into that sort of thing.

"Are you the club peeper?" I asked him.

His face was a rock with eyebrows. "If you mean, am I in charge of security, then yes, I am. The name's Baxter. Jonathan Augustus Baxter."

He had a big wrinkly sunburned face, like a professional shark-hunter, and bright blue eyes that looked like two rubies dropped on the ocean sand.

"What's a two-bit private eye like you doing in a place like this?" he said, and I couldn't help thinking that it sounded like a bad pick-up line in a Marx Brothers movie:

Let's go somewhere we can be alone. Ah, there doesn't seem to be anyone on this couch.

"I'm working a case," I told him.

His eyebrows crawled to where his hairline would have been if he'd had any hair. "Ah, so you're investigating Robert Barrett's murder?"

"I never said anything about Robert Barrett. How did you know that?"

"I can read, Mr. Brand. It's been all over the papers." He had an odor of sweat, bay rum, and Woodbury after-shaving powder. "What do you expect to find here at the club? Surely not the murderer?"

"You never know what you might find in a joint like this," I said with a shrug. "Did you know Barrett well, Mr. Baxter?"

"Of course I knew him. I know everyone who is a member of the club."

"What was he like?"

"He was a fine man and a faithful husband and not a bad golfer on top of it."

"A real pillar of society, huh? Did you know Barrett had a chippie on the side? Tall juicy blonde with nice ample teats. She had the misfortune of getting boxed too."

"You're vulgar, Mr. Brand."

"And you smell. Know the girl, Baxter?"

He let out a short harsh laugh, which made no change in the hard lines of his face. He picked up my wallet from the desk and threw it at me.

"Go home, Mr. Brand. You got the wrong map, kid, and no light to read it by."

"Kid? Who you calling kid? I'm old enough to be...I don't know; I'm old enough to be something. Hell, I'm old."

"Just get out of here, Brand. Go home and lay dormy for a while. Put on some music, sit by the fire, pour yourself some grog. But don't let me find you peddling your wares around the club."

Grog? Did he really just say grog?

His teeth were as white as the pearl of a gun butt. "Do we understand one another, Mr. Brand?"

I rubbed the place behind my ear where he had sapped me. "Yeah, I understand. I understand quite well."

"Good." Baxter stubbed out his smelly cigarette and smiled his big-toothed smile at me again. "I do have to give it to you, Mr. Brand, you know when to listen. I like you."

I smiled back at him. I was glad he liked me because I knew he didn't like me very much. But I was one up on him; I didn't like him at all.

"Goodbye, Mr. Brand."

I stood up and slipped my hat on, careful not to hit the place where he'd sapped me. "Yeah, see ya around."

I got out of that closet and started looking for the nearest exit. It was at the end of the long glass corridor. At the other end was the club bar room, directly across the hall from the ballroom. People dressed in their finest glad rags were coming out of that expansive ballroom and dipping into the little bar.

I thought about Baxter's warnings. Then I walked down the glass corridor toward the bar. Screw Baxter. He was nothing more than a club dick with an oversized ego.

I went into the bar, sat down among the lounging aristocrats and burgeoning millionaires, went up to the bar and ordered a beer. In a place like this it would only cost me one arm and part of a leg.

The bartender glared at my shabby suit and my battered face. "You a member, Barney?"

I took out my wallet and put a sawbuck on top of the bar. There was something about Alexander Hamilton's face that the bartender liked.

He looked around to make sure no one was watching, then he picked up Hamilton and poured me a clean good-looking tap beer, and I handed him another sawbuck to keep them coming.

I sat there and sipped my beer. It was good and clean; something I wasn't used to. Something imported.

The millionaire elbow-crookers at the other end of the bar finished their martinis and went back into the ballroom.

There were only a few other people left in the bar, sitting at red-draped tables in the back. Johnny Mercer was being pumped through the expensive sound system, singing "Strip Poker."

I dragged out my Luckies, flipped one loose and listened as Mercer moved on to "I Lost My Sugar In Salt Lake City."

I kept looking at the door expecting Jonathan Augustus Baxter to come rushing in and throw me out, but he never materialized.

Then a bird putting the push on fifty came in and sat down at the bar next to me. She was wearing some kind of expensive animal wrapped around her bare shoulders and a jade green evening gown and a fortune of ice flashing on her fingers and neck. She had on more diamonds than I had ever seen before, outside of a jewelry-store window.

I waved the bartender over and asked the bediamoned woman what she was drinking.

"Sidecar," she said.

She was almost fifty, but she still had her looks. Good dark looks that only money can buy, with a mass of curly blue-black hair, a rather sullen face that must have been extremely pretty once, and eyes as empty and beautiful as a Greek bust. Just another rich, lonely bluestocking.

I picked up my beer and saluted her.

"My name's Elston," I said. "Elston Brand."

She held out her ornamented hand. "Mary Bannister."

"Nice to meet you, Mary Bannister."

"Likewise." She sipped her sidecar and looked at me sideways. "What happened to your face, Mr. Brand?"

I'd almost forgotten about my face—the bruise over my eye compliments of Jimmy and Leo, the swollen lip and the gash on my cheek thrown in for good measure. Not to mention the gorge on the side of my head that Baxter had most recently given me.

"I got into a wrestling match with a bear," I told Mary Bannister. "The bear won."

Mary Bannister laughed. "You're silly. There aren't any bears left in California." She stopped and took a stare at my threadbare suit. "What do you do for a living, Mr. Brand?"

"Guess."

She eyed me more closely over the rim of her sidecar and her dark eyes did pretty things. "You don't look like a cop, but you don't look like a man who is not a cop. You have marks on you."

"Private."

"I beg pardon?"

"I'm a private dick," I told her.

Her eyes stayed on my face. "You've had a violent life, haven't you, Mr. Brand?"

"More than most."

She was silent for a little while, then she asked: "Are you here investigating a case?"

"Yes, I am."

"Maybe I'm talking too much," she said.

"Maybe not enough," I said.

She moved her head a little toward me, and spoke out of the side of her mouth like a prison con. "Robert Barrett's murder?"

I nodded my head in silent affirmation, feeling like Joseph Cotton in an Orson Wells movie.

"Everyone is talking about it," she said. "Gossiping like little girls. It just makes me sick!"

"Did you know Robert Barrett?" I asked.

"Oh yes. Quite well, in fact. He was a partner in my husband's firm for a while, before he went on to public work. My husband is a lawyer, I'm afraid." She giggled, her voice starting to slur a little. "No one likes lawyers, and neither do I. I just happened to marry one."

I pointed at her glass; it was nearly empty already.

"Care for another?" I asked.

"Oh yes," she said, without hesitation.

I waved the bartender over. I gave him another sawbuck and he smiled at me like I was John D. Rockefeller.

Mary Bannister got her new drink and took a nice long swallow. "I can't stand these things," she said. At first I thought she was talking about the drink, but the way she was slinging them back didn't make any sense.

"These stupid fundraisers," she went on, indicating the crowded ballroom. "Everyone trying to impress everyone else. I wish I was at home with my kids playing checkers and roasting chestnuts.

Have you ever roasted a chestnut? Do people actually even roast chestnuts anymore?"

"What was Robert like?" I asked, wanting to get to her before the drinks she was sucking down did. I felt like a down-and-out private dick, a buffoon clutching at straws, which is exactly what I was.

"I hate to speak poorly of the dead," Mary Bannister said, "but when Robert died they didn't have to embalm him. The fluid already ran in his veins. Oh, I shouldn't. But...Robert liked his power and kind of held it over everyone else's head, including his wife. Poor little thing."

I got excited and my heart started beating like Buddy Bolden's trumpet.

"How well did you know his wife?" I asked.

"Melissa? She used to come around the club a lot in the old days. Not so much now." She licked some lipstick off her teeth and took another swallow of her sidecar. "Missy was awfully young when she first met Robert. I always thought of her as the deer in the headlights. You know what I mean, Mr. Brand?"

I sipped my beer and noticed a rather short, rather pudgy man come into the bar. He was wearing a perfectly tailored penguin suit; short and fat and trying to wear that penguin suit like he was tall and slim. He had a swarthy tan, which either had to be inherited or fake, and a black beard that was so dark it looked dyed. There's something about a man with a beard that I can't stand. No particular reason for it. Prejudice, I suppose some people might call it. But I felt the same way about asparagus.

The penguin looked around, saw Mary at the bar and waddled over furiously. "There you are! I've been looking all over for you, Mary! You're missing the party."

There was a trace of accent in his voice. It was cultured, but definitely foreign. He was looking at me now; at my shabby suit and shabby coat and shabby tie. That's the way it is in the United States these days. A native born American can't make a decent living and here was a blow-in all set to tell me what was wrong with me.

"Who is this man?" the penguin asked, nodding his head at me.

Mary Bannister smiled rather rakishly at him. "This is Elston Brand. He's a private detective."

I held out my hand but the penguin didn't take it. He just looked at me like I was some kind of specimen in a cage.

"I don't care who he is. He could be Jesus Christ himself. I want you back in that party, Mary! Now!"

"Lay off, pops," I told him. "The lady's enjoying a drink. Well, several of them actually."

He glared at me. "Oh, I'm sorry, did I interrupt you? I didn't mean to interrupt you." He puffed out his chest, prohibitively with indignation, but still couldn't get it past his considerable belly. "Do you know who I am, sir? I can have you thrown out. In fact, I could have you arrested for trespassing. Who are you anyway? What are you doing here? And why are you speaking to my wife?"

I sipped my beer and said in a very tired, distant voice, "Don't bark and show your teeth at me unless you plan to bite, fatso!"

Mary couldn't help giggling, and she let out a little burp.

The penguin got all flustered and his fat face got red up to his hairline. He made an abrupt, angry motion. His eyes glittered. The corners of his pink mouth drew down and an oversized tongue made a quick pass over his lips.

An angry flush pumped more color into his phthisical cheeks. He sneered at me with his expressive nostrils. "How dare you! You—you—you—"

Goddamn; that pretentious fat face of his was making me madder every second I had to look at it.

"Go back to the party, Joseph," Mary finally told him, perhaps sensing my irritability. "I'll be there in a minute."

The penguin huffed and puffed for another minute, and then he pouted his way out of the bar and went back into the adjoining ballroom. Meanwhile, Mary was draining the last of her third sidecar like a Little Leaguer gulps grape-flavored Kool-Aid after a long hot ball game.

"Care for one more?" I asked her.

"Oh, I better not," she said, blushing. Then: "Oh what the hell? You only live once, right? What's that old saying? *Do what thou will shall be the whole of the law?* I guess one more won't kill me."

I had no idea what she was talking about, but I bought her a fresh drink and sat back to listen to her squawk some more.

"Missy was always good-humored," she went on. "Missy loved life and loved everybody...And how she used to laugh. She was quite beautiful in a sort of beachcomber way. All the old men in the club used to follow her around like stupid dogs, their eyes glazed and their tongues wagging. In some funny way I was jealous of her, but I liked her a lot. She told me once that she had been born on a horse farm near Isle Vista. She had a close friend from high school and they left Isle Vista shortly after graduation. They got jobs waitressing in Long Beach. She told me once that she became pregnant. Some young sailor whom she met and quickly left her. Sometimes a young girl runs into unfortunate circumstances. You know what I mean, Mr. Brand? They do what they have to do. I really got the impression that she hated men then. But Robert wanted her from the very first moment he laid his eyes on her, and there was nothing stopping Robert from getting what he wanted. Missy was naïve, I guess. She had no friends or family, except an older brother who had been killed when she was young. She told me she had been very fond of him. Almost like a father-figure. She told me she was almost hopeless after he was murdered. She was all on her own."

"Melissa had a brother?"

"Yes."

Melissa never told me she had a brother. The whole thing was like a jigsaw puzzle, except every now and then a round peg appeared and didn't fit the square hole.

I was letting it all sink in when I saw Jonathan Augustus Baxter out in the corridor. The penguin was talking to him.

Suddenly, Baxter pursed his lips like a man about to spit out a prune pit and he came storming into the bar.

"Brand!" he hollered, pushing over a barstool in his reckless pursuit of me. "I thought I told you to take a powder!"

I threw a pickle at him from someone's Bloody Mary and made a Groucho Marx dash to the exit and out the door, jerking past Baxter's outstretched hand with my head turned the other way.

I flew down the marble-faced steps, and shot across the parking lot and into my Electra, but of course it wouldn't start on the first try.

It never does. Just like the movies when someone's in hot pursuit of our favorite victim and the damn car won't start.

The motor coughed, spluttered. I yanked out the choke button. The motor fired, missed again; the cylinders pumping with furious emptiness.

Baxter was slowly making ground, but I finally got the Electra going on the third try.

The gears kicked in, the car jumped forward, and I peeled out of there with the receding dark figure of Jonathan Augustus Baxter screaming at me in the rear-view mirror.

Chapter Twenty-six

I let my hands and my eyes drive me back to town while the rest of me fingered out the bits and pieces like a puzzle, until there was only one little piece left.

Melissa had a brother.

For a minute I was back in her big bedroom with the wild taste of her in my mouth as we tumbled around stainless white sheets.

I had to find her.

I had to find out what happened. Time was getting shorter by the second.

    Time,

        time,

            time...

The race of hours, of minutes, of seconds...

I pounded on the horn at the old guy in the Packard clogging up traffic in front of me on Cahuenga and screamed at him as I pulled around him.

On Beverly Boulevard I found a saloon with an empty parking place right out in front. I went in and threw a buck on the bar. When my beer came I took a nickel from the change and wormed into a phone booth down the end and dialed operator.

When she cut in I asked for the Fifth Precinct. There were some clicks as the connection was completed.

It was late, but Rudy wasn't a guy to hold to absolute schedules and I was lucky this time.

I said, "Hey, Rudy, remember me?"

He laughed into the receiver. "Hell, Elston, with all your publicity how could I forget you?"

"How's the cop business?"

"Booming, Elston, really booming."

I let a few seconds go by. "What's the word on Barrett's bodyguard? Did Frank ever find him?"

Rudy's breathing came heavy over the receiver. "A pickup went out on him yesterday. As far as the Santa Rita P.D. is concerned he disappeared completely."

Some elusive little thing flashed across my mind and my eyes twisted into a squint as I tried to catch it.

Real softly I said, "What do you know about a hood named Joey Chill?"

"Small time. Used to deal heroin out of Laguna Beach. Got mixed up with Barrett somehow, and a year later turned up dead."

"Did he have any aliases, other than Joey Chill I mean?"

"Hold on, I'll check."

Rudy put down the receiver and I could hear him open a file cabinet. I squeezed the phone in my fist and looked around. The after-supper crowd began drifting in and taking places at the bar.

"Here it is," Rudy said when he came back on the line. "Joey Chill, alias Joey Fingers, alias Joey

Doves, alias Joey Agnello, alias Joey DeVito, alias Joey...*Sparrow*."

It was like something cold trickling into my ear from the receiver. Suddenly I couldn't open my mouth, or lift a hand or think. I tasted my heart up there in my throat and I wanted to spit.

Joey Chill was Melissa's brother?

It didn't make any sense.

"Elston...you still there?...Elston...?"

"Yeah, I'm here, Rudy."

The strands of the web began to join together, and little by little, piece by piece, the thing that was possible became probable.

"You okay, man?" Rudy asked.

I grunted an assent. "Thanks for the information, Rudy."

"Hey, no skin off my nose."

I cradled the receiver and went back to the bar and finished my beer, my mind going round and round in the squirrel cage.

It was like a tangled skein of fish line, hard to figure out where in the snarl lay the end and the beginning.

I was playing all the angles against each other until I was getting all juiced up with crazy ideas, and that wasn't good. I didn't have time for crazy ideas, and they sure as hell weren't helping me get any closer to finding Melissa.

I knew she had been in my apartment the night Robert lost his head—in more ways than one. I made her take a drink and lie down in my bed while I went hell-bent to his office.

What happened to her after that?

Chapter Twenty-seven

Outside the night had a weird buzzing to it and the heat was back with a vengeance. It was more curiosity than anything else that put me on Telegraph Road. I went there without any precise motive. There was just a chance that I might stumble on something that I had so far overlooked.

When I got to the Barrett mansion I cruised around a little to see if the buttons had a police shadow on the place. I turned the corner, took up a station in the shadows, and waited for an interminable interval. Then I did a u-turn up the block and drove past the house. It was big and dark and ominous. Everything looked so calm, so prosperous; so unsuspicious.

I parked the Electra behind a heavy clump of Manzanita and ironwood, grabbed the big nickel flash out of the glove, and crossed the street. I walked slowly along the high brick fence, keeping myself in the shadows. The gate was locked. I'd have to climb it.

I stuck the flashlight in the waistband of my pants and scaled the fence at the corner, moving slowly, trying not to make noise. It was difficult getting a grip with the tips of my shoes and I slipped a few times, but eventually I got a firm hold with one of my toes and was able to hoist myself over the top.

I landed hard on the other side, and crouched there, waiting, listening. I could hear the ocean crashing somewhere far in the distance, but there was no sound, no movement around the house.

I brought my flash into play, following its wan direction in and out among the looming, ghostly ornamental trees surrounding the front entrance.

The place was locked up, tight and dark.

I went around the side and along a patio with a large oblong pool framed in a patchwork of colored tiles. I knew there would be security linked to the house and the electric wires weren't too hard to find. The wires cut easily.

Then I held my hat against the glass panel of the back door and smashed the pane with my elbow. Glass fell tinkling lightly inside.

I slipped my hand through the glass-toothed opening, careful not to cut myself on the shards, and turned the lock and the deadbolt.

Inside, I swished the flashlight around. The kitchen was large and shiny and looked like it wasn't used much. A short hall led to the living room. Paintings on the wall—originals by Breughel—stared down at me; *The Adoration of the Kings, The Triumph of Death, The Land of Cockayne;* gloomy little things.

The house spoke in tones of eerie silence. It was so deserted-feeling now, so patently lifeless. I wondered if Robert Barrett's ghost was watching me.

It was easy to see that the police had been over everything in the place. They had gone at it efficiently. Everything was replaced much the same as it had been. There were just a few things not quite in order that made it possible to tell that it had been searched.

I climbed the stairs leading up to the second floor, shined the flash, and went down the hall to the bedroom.

I lifted the mattress and felt along the seams for any possible opening or place where it may have been stitched up, hoping to find Barrett's money or the heroin. I even tried the window shades, thinking that something—anything—might have been rolled up in one of them.

On the dresser, there was a photo of Melissa when she was a kid, maybe eleven or twelve years old, on the beach wearing an Easter-egg blue dress and a pink frilly hat with her long black hair hanging out of it. She was standing in the sunlight, her eyes squinted against the sun and she stood pigeon-toed, with her hands behind her back. There was something of the tomboy in her, but if you looked at the eyes, you could almost see the vamp she would later become.

I opened one of the dresser drawers. It was full of puffy sweaters and white cotton socks. I dug around in there, but I might as well not have taken the time. Nothing.

I opened another drawer. It was a jumble of female unmentionables; tangled skeins of silk stockings and fluttery lace with twined straps and underwire cups.

I emptied the bottom drawer and a pair of purple frilly knickers caught and slipped over the back. I pulled the drawer all the way out and found a passport under the plywood bottom. In the photo

Melissa was wearing a linen dress and a Panama hat.

I put the passport in my pocket and looked around one last time. Then I went back into the hallway and down the stairs, through the kitchen and out the back door into the warm windy night.

Outside, the gardens had a haunted look, as though small wild eyes were watching me from behind the bushes, as though the moon itself was hiding something in its light.

I swiped the flashlight across the yard and cut through the bands of thickening shadow. Then I went up and over the fence again and landed in a crouch on the other side.

The Electra was still sitting by itself in the shadows behind the Manzanita and ironwood. I walked quickly to the car and got in, and that's when I saw him in the backseat.

He was sitting there in the darkness, his bloodshot eyes never leaving mine, and a puff of smoke shot out of his thin lips.

"Jesus, Frank!" I said, catching my breath. "You scared three days worth of growth out of me."

His steely eyes shone like silver scales, his thin smoker lips parted in a sort of rigid half smile.

"What are you doing here, Elston?" he said in a voice like iced velvet. "What, no wise cracks this time? What were you looking for?"

I didn't answer him. I didn't know how to answer him.

"C'mon, Elston, you're behind the eight-ball here. You're already on our radar for Barrett's murder, now I've got you for breaking and entering, on top of everything else. I'm no lawyer, but I got to think this wouldn't be too good for your defense. People on a jury might think you came here trying to cover something up."

I knew I had to tell him something. So, for once in my life I told the truth. "Look, Frank, I was trying to find something—anything—that might tell me where Melissa is."

"That's better," Frank said, smiling now with his silver smoker's eyes. "And what did you find?"

"Nothing. I swear."

He reached into the long herringbone overcoat he was wearing and took out a small .22. I could see its shiny barrel in the darkness. It wasn't his usual .45 service pistol.

I laughed. But it was one of those nervous little laughs that didn't mean much.

"What are you going to do with that thing, Frank, shoot me?"

I laughed again, but his countenance hadn't changed and that started to worry me a little. For a moment I thought he might actually shoot me in the back of the head and leave me out there.

"I didn't find anything," I told him. "I swear to you, Frank."

This time it was his turn to laugh. It was amazing how he could laugh without moving his colorless lips.

"You're hiding something from me, Elston. And that makes me very angry. Now, I want you to tell your old friend Frank what you're hiding."

"I don't know what the hell you're talking about."

He leaned on the seat behind my head and pressed the barrel of the gun against my neck. I could smell his hot smelly breath on my skin. That's when I started to really believe he was going to shoot me. Leave me there on the dark street with a .22 slug in my skull.

"Whoever killed Barrett that night was looking for something in his office," Frank said, talking to me confidentially, but it was the gun he had pressed against my neck that was doing all the talking. "I think you know *what* that something is. I think you came here trying to find that certain something. And you're going to tell your old friend Frank what that certain something is, or I'm going to blow your fucking head off."

"What do you gain by shooting me, Frank?"

"I gain a killer."

"C'mon, you know I didn't kill Barrett. I wanted to, but someone beat me to it."

"It don't really matter who killed him, Elston. Either way, I get the credit for bringing down Barrett's murderer."

I had to call his bluff. It was my only play.

"You're not going to shoot me, Frank."

"You got a better idea?"

"I've got lots of ideas, Frank."

"Let's hear them."

"Barrett was dealing heroin. Whoever killed him sold it on the streets. For a lot of money. Let me snoop around a little more. See what I turn up."

"How much is a lot of money?"

"A quarter of a mill a lot."

Little tight lines seemed to grow around Frank's eyes. "Did you find any of the dough in the house?"

"Does it look like I did? Does it look like I'm carrying around a half a million dollars, Frank?"

"Don't get cocky. You're still not out of the woods, Elston. I still might shoot you." Then his voice went someplace faraway. "A quarter mill, huh? That's a lot of money no one knows about."

I could almost see the wheels churning in that thick head of his.

"I never figured you for a *dirty* cop, Frank."

"Do you know how much a *clean* cop on salary takes home a year, Elston?"

"Nope, but it's more than me, I'd guess."

Frank shrugged. "That may be, but it's still nothing to write home about. I've been on the force for almost twenty years. I'm getting old. I got a wife and three kids to think about. What do you got?"

"My pride."

He laughed. "How far did your pride get you when Kitty Carlisle was being sliced up like a Thanksgiving turkey?"

I still didn't feel good about that. "I can find the money, Frank." I told him. "I'll find the cash and you'll get *thirty percent* and you'll get your killer. You'll be a hero on the force and get thirty percent of a quarter mill. How does that sound?"

"Thirty percent, Elston? What happens to the rest?"

"Call it a finder's fee. It's only fair if I do all the work."

He smiled and the creases around his lip-less mouth turned into deep hollows. "What makes you think I can't do it myself? Just shoot you right here, right now and find the money and the killer myself?"

"You haven't found him yet."

He thought about that for a minute.

"Fifty percent," he said.

"Forty."

He pressed the gun harder into the back of my neck. "Fifty. Or I kill you now and finger you for Barrett's murder."

"Alright, fifty."

"Good. Then we've got a deal." The pressure of the gun on my neck relaxed. "But if you cross me, you'll end up wearing a D.O.A. tag on your big toe."

"What about that bull cop of yours?" I asked.

"Updike? What about him?"

"How much does he know about all this?"

"Ron's got elephant ears. He does what I tell him. He's straight muscle all the way. No imagination. No guts. Working with elbows like Updike every day is like being stuck behind a slow driver in rush hour traffic. Life moves fast, Elston. You got to learn to move with it. Take the opportunities that are presented to you."

"Is that what you call it, Frank?"

He sat back in the seat and slipped the gun back in his coat, smiling like a drunken undertaker the whole time.

"Just remember, Elston, you've got a tail. So don't even think about running off with the money yourself. You make a move toward a bus, train, or an airplane, and you'll find your ass behind bars, or worse. You got me?"

"I need Uptight off my back," I told him. "He's on me like a bad hemorrhoid I can't get rid of. I need to move about and I can't have Uptight sniffing at my heels all the time."

"Ron was just doing what I told him."

"*You* stuck him on me?"

"Of course."

"Did you see what he did to my face?"

Frank leaned across the seat, grabbed the back of my head and stared at my pieced-together mug.

"Don't worry, it'll heal and you'll be just as ugly as always."

He opened the back door and slid out of the car like the snake he was. I looked in the rear view and watched as he slithered away to find whatever rock he had crawled out from under.

Chapter Twenty-eight

When Frank was gone I lit a cigarette and sat in the car for a while, thinking and staring down the hill at the ships in the bay at San Pedro.

On the horizon the lights were draped across the sky like a blanket.

The heat was on. I had to find Melissa or my old *friend* Frank was going to kill me. Melissa was the key piece to this whole puzzle.

Where could she be hiding?

It was going on a week now, and no one had seen hide nor hair of her. She could be anywhere in the world. And it's a big world.

I knew she wasn't stupid enough to try to take a plane or train out of Santa Rita. The buttons had been tracking any departures out since the day Barrett was blipped.

So where was she?

Suddenly that little finger poking at my brain thumped a couple pieces together that made lovely, beautiful sense.

I smiled and drove down the mountain to the local Greyhound station on Fifth and Vine. Every night a northbound bus left Santa Rita for Summerland, Montecito, San Buenaventura, and *Isle Vista* at twelve-fifteen. A bus was as inconspicuous a way for Melissa to get out of town as any.

I went into the station and found a driver in the lounge having coffee and a sandwich. He was a short fat guy with eyebrows that met above his nose and a scrimy little goatee that waggled when he talked and made his chin come to a point.

I asked him if he had been the driver on that run the night Robert Barrett was killed, last Thursday.

He asked me why I wanted to know. I made up a lie, but he saw through it and wanted ten bucks.

I gave him the ten bucks.

He put down his sandwich, took a tattered bus schedule out of his pocket, looked at it for a second and said, yeah, he was the driver that night, what of it?

I asked him if he remembered any specific people on that trip and he looked at me as if I had purple spots.

"I drive a helluva lot of busses, Mac."

"You'd remember this passenger," I said, taking out Melissa's passport and showing it to him. "Black hair and green eyes that would stop a Sherman tank."

He started to shake his head slowly and then stopped shaking it.

He held out his hand. I gave him another ten.

"I don't know if this is anything or not," he said. "But as I was making my Summerland stop and somewhere after that, this little car goes by me doing a hundred, maybe a hundred ten. Up ahead it slows down and I had to pass it. Then it goes by me again doing a hundred. Looked like a girl driving. She had blonde hair, not black like you said, but I didn't get a good look at her. Pretty enough though, I could tell you that. The third time she whizzed past me, she laid on the horn like she was trying to flag someone down."

"Someone on the bus?"

"That's what it looked like to me."

"What happened then?"

"When I got to Isle Vista the car was waiting there in the parking lot. Does this help at all?"

"Yeah."

I added another ten to what he already had, and then I got back in my car and drove to my apartment.

I had twenty-five blocks to go, and it was still hot out, though not as oppressively muggy as it had been the last few days. I was in no hurry to be alone in the apartment. Out here, on the street, I could think about the heat and the taxicabs and the fairies lined up along Canal Street, looking hopefully with gray-tinged round eyes at all the men hurrying by. I could think about Robert Barrett and Kitty Carlisle. I could think about Bedbug Santucci and Dominick and Theresa Kramer and half a million other things.

In the apartment, I would only be able to think of Melissa.

But I always go home. Always. I may sometimes detour, but eventually I get there.

The St. Pauli girl smiled down at me from her perch on the billboard. I dreamed of climbing up between those two enormous breasts of hers and falling asleep there for a week or two. But I couldn't. I had work to do.

I climbed the rickety staircase like a puppet dangling from slack strings. A light bracketed against the wall—drooping upside-down like a withered tulip in its bell-shaped shade of scalloped glass—cast a smoky yellow glow.

I unlocked the door to my darkened room, and went inside.

Whoever hit me didn't even give me a chance to take my hat off.

I didn't see the punch, but I felt it on my chin like a sledgehammer.

I let out a little sound like "*unck!*" and fell to the floor like a new bride's nightie.

My assailant's voice was a lazy thread stitching through the shadows:

"I heard you been looking for me, milquetoast."

I rolled over on the floor and looked up to see Dominick staring down at me. He looked like King Kong.

Before he could hit me again, I reached out and kicked him in the shins, and he let out a scream like the whinny of a horse.

I tried to get to my feet, but he was fast for his size. He picked me up by my chest and threw me halfway across the room where I landed on my poor little kitchen table and it shattered into several pieces of kindling.

I rolled around on the hard linoleum for a while, and then staggered to my feet.

Dominick was standing there in front of me, ready to break me in half. In his left hand he was holding a switch that looked like a saber. Apparently, after he was done breaking me in half, he was going to disembowel me, too.

My mouth twisted into a bloody lopsided smile. "So that's how you want to play, huh, Aunt Jemima?"

That got him.

He started snorting and I swear to God I saw smoke coming out of his flaring nostrils.

He came charging at me like a bull I once saw at a bullfight down in Juarez. I *ole'd* him and kicked the knife out of his left hand and it went sliding into the dusty wasteland under the couch.

He looked surprised for a second, and then he lowered his head and put his shoulder into my midsection. It felt like I had just been tackled by Clyde "Bulldog" Turner and I could feel the wind going out of me as I tumbled over the battered sofa and landed on the floor.

Dominick picked me up and put me in a bear hold. The man had a grip that could crack a telephone pole.

I reached up and grabbed the back of his head and drove my forehead into his face.

He stumbled back holding his bloody nose.

"How do you like it?" I sneered.

He came back at me with a left hook that caught me by surprise and split my nose in half. He followed it up with a right to my ribs.

I crawled over the fallen sofa and before he got a chance to hit me again I slapped him with a pillow, but that didn't do any good.

He grabbed me and put me in a headlock and used his right hand to pry my lips apart.

"What you want with me, ditchpig?" he growled.

It was hard to answer him with his fingers in my mouth, but I managed to say, "Where were you the night Robert Barrett was killed?" It sounded more like, "Wha u new nigh Bear kill?"

He flipped me over his shoulder and I landed hard on the hardwood floor.

"I was at home watching *Howdy Doody*," he said.

I rolled over, grabbed a chair, and hit him in the chest with it.

It didn't even faze him. He looked down at his chest and wiped away the bits of broken chair.

"I'm gonna kill you!"

He picked me up and put me in another bear hold. It felt like my whole body was put in a vice and the life was being sucked out of me.

"I had no part in Mister Barrett's killing," he said, breathing chicken livers all over my face.

I got my arms free and boxed his ears.

He let me go and I took a second to get the life flowing back in me. Then I gave him an uppercut to the chin. It felt like I broke two knuckles, but it did the job.

Dominick stumbled back like a drunk, and then fell on his back like a tree that has been chopped down. The room shook when he hit the floor.

"Where's Melissa?" I said, standing over him.

He didn't answer, so I kicked him in the ribs.

"*Where is she!*"

"I don't know," he moaned. "I haven't seen her since it happened."

I tried to kick him again, but he grabbed my foot and flipped me over.

He got to his feet quickly. Like I said, he moved fast for a big man.

He grabbed me by the belt of my pants and threw me headfirst into the wall.

My head left a gaping hole in the sheetrock. (My landlord was going to take that out of the damage deposit I'd put on the place.)

Alright. Now I was starting to get angry. All that time gone to waste, I thought. I had been playing it soft when I should have played it hard.

There had been enough words. Now the fun ought to start.

I stood up and we squared off like two roosters ready to leap and slash with the spurs.

He threw a right cross. I blocked it with my left shoulder.

He threw a left. I ducked and came up swinging.

I caught him in the gut with a right and got him in the jaw with a left hook and felt my knuckles rip open when I got him in the mouth.

He looked confused for a second, and then he dropped to his knees. I grabbed the back of his head with both hands and drove my thigh into his nose and he fell to the floor face first with his arms flung out wide.

I straddled his back like a man riding a wild animal and put my left arm around his throat.

"Where is she!"

"I don't know," he coughed, the spit dripping down his bloody chin.

"You were hired to watch Barrett's back. Someone paid you to scratch early the night he was blipped." I tightened my grip on his throat. "Who was it? Was it Melissa? Where is she?"

"I told you I don't know."

I used my right hand to rake his eyes.

"Ouch! Okay, okay. She paid me a hundred bucks to leave early that night."

"Where is she?"

"I don't know."

I raked his eyes again.

"Ah, man! I don't know."

"You better think of something, or I'm gonna break your neck."

"Okay, okay. I heard her talkin' on the phone that night. She mentioned somthin' about Isle Vista. She might be there. That's all I know."

I grabbed an empty bottle of V.O. off the floor and hit him over the head with it. The lights went out in his eyes and his face hit the floor again, an inert mass. Pretty soon he was snoring like all three-thirds of the Three Stooges.

I stood up and looked down at him. He looked like a big bear rug lying there on my floor.

"No hard feelings," I said.

Stiff-legged and stiff-shouldered, I dragged myself into the bathroom, bleeding all over the place.

I looked in the mirror. My left eye was mush and my nose was lying on the other side of my face.

I couldn't do anything about my eye, but I rearranged my nose and then went into the bedroom, poked around in the closet, packed my single suitcase with my extra-wrinkled suit, two pairs of socks, my last white shirt and a couple of pairs of boxers with more holes in them than a golf course.

I needed some money and I needed to get to Isle Vista. I still had a lot of what Melissa and Robert had given me, but I needed more. I took what was left out of my sock drawer and shoved it in my wallet.

Frank and his boys were watching out for my Electra and I needed to roam without them knowing about it. So I left Dominick lying there in my kitchen and hoofed it a couple of blocks to *Able Car Repair and Tires*. My unfriendly neighborhood mechanic, Dirty Ernie, was under a jacked-up chassis of an old Ford, letting out the drain plug.

Ernie frequently spoke to his cars as if they were his lovers: "C'mon, you old bitch, piss on me!

"Hey, Ernie," I called out.

He slid out from under the Ford and gave me a toothless smile, his face so thick with grease that he looked like Al Jolson in *The Jazz Singer*.

"Elston Brand? Is that you?"

"In the flesh."

He looked at my battered face. "You can say that again."

His clothes were gray, stained coveralls and a torn work shirt with ERNIE written in cursive over his left breast.

"You still owe me fifty bucks from when I did your brakes, Elston."

I took out my wallet and gave him seventy-five.

He looked at it like it was *Monopoly* money. "Is it real?"

"It's real," I said.

"I'd ask where you got it, but I don't think I want to know."

"I need a car, Ernie. Just for a few days. I need to get out of town and the cops have a shadow on my Electra."

He looked around the cluttered garage. "I got this one," he said, pointing at a lonely prohibition-era Model-T in the corner. It was older than the Pyramids and Stonehenge combined.

"That's all you got, Ernie?"

"Beggars can't be choosers, Elston."

I flipped him another Jackson for the trouble. "I'll have it back in a few days."

Chapter Twenty-nine

Before I got on the road to Isle Vista I had one more stop. I went in among the wan, hopeless faces that were raised to me at the bar. Empty eye sockets staring up at me with no light behind them.

Angie's voice came at me like a spell from behind the bar:

"Hello, stranger."

"Hello, sweetheart."

"How're you feeling?"

"Hot."

"Have a beer, it'll cool you down."

"I'm not talking about that kind of heat. I'm up to my ear flaps in trouble, Ang. This is one week they can tear out of the calendar and throw away."

I sipped my beer and lit a cigarette for both of us. Angie took a long inhale and let the smoke out in two streams through her nostrils. She looked me over.

"What happened to your face this time?"

I ran my fingers gently over my broken nose. "The private eye business isn't the gravy train with biscuit wheels I had hoped for. People seem to get annoyed when I'm around."

"I don't."

"Thanks, sweetheart."

Her lips were like cherries and she smelled like Root Beer Fizz. "So—do the cops still think you bopped that big-shot lawyer?"

"Yeah," I said. "Crazy, isn't it?"

She didn't say anything. I looked up at her.

"You believe I didn't kill him, don't you, Ang?"

"Do you read, Elston?"

"Yeah, I read," I said, a bit too defensively.

"Ever read a book called *Sappho?*"

I looked at her like she was nuts.

"The hero had strong obligations. A job, a good family. And all he had to gain by his discretions was a woman of easy virtue. She was an unbelievably beautiful woman of easy virtue, but aren't we all when someone falls in love with us?"

I had no idea what she was talking about.

"There's a blind spot in all of us, Elston. Sometimes apples can be as tart as they are sweet."

A group of rowdy sailors came in and sat at the other end of the bar. Angie went over to serve them. While I waited for her to come back I heard a young couple sitting at a table behind me talking about a sea otter parasite that was killing the little buggers up in Resurrection Bay. It seems some people were flushing cat feces down the toilet, infecting the clams that the sea otters eat. And I thought I was having a bad day. Hell, on a day like this you could be depressed by the message in a fortune cookie.

Angie finished serving the sailors and came back to stand in front of me.

"Do you like kids, Elston?"

"Who's kids?" I asked, taking the weed out of my mouth for a bit of fresh air.

"Anybody's kids. Kids."

"Yeah, I guess. Why?"

She had a faraway look in her eyes. "No reason."

I snuffed the cigarette. "I'm leaving town for a few days, Ang."

"Where are you going?"

"Place called Isle Vista."

"What are you going to do in Isle Vista?"

"I'm gonna close the case I'm working on," I told her. "How's the new boyfriend?"

"The doctor?"

"Yeah, the doctor."

"We broke up."

"Why?"

She shrugged. Her body did very pretty things when she shrugged. "He wanted more than I wanted to give. Same old story."

"One day me and you—"

She held up a hand. "Don't say it unless you really mean it."

"How do you know I don't really mean it?"

"We've been around that block before, Elston."

Right then I thought she was the most beautiful woman in the world. And I told her so.

She batted her mascaraed eyes at me and cooed, "Yeah, well, we'll see about that when you get back from Isle Vista. Give 'em hell, Elston."

I put on my hat and headed for the door.

"Don't take any new lovers until I get back."

Chapter Thirty

It took about three hours to drive up to Isle Vista. I got there a little after four in the morning, with a high hard sky glaring down and the temperature still in the upper-eighties.

Isle Vista was a beach town, noted for tourists, white sand, an old Spanish mission, and tourists. Nothing else.

I pulled the old Ford, nose in, on the parking apron in front of the first cheap motel I saw.

A battered sign on the roof said THE MODERN AIRE—30 ROOMS SOME WITH BATH. OPEN YEAR ROU D.

I parked the car, got out, dragged out my suitcase, and walked into the small dirty lobby.

Behind the desk was a fat woman with a couple chins whose cheap flowered dress stuck to her in the heat. A big floor fan was wasting its time in the center of the room.

"Room," I snapped. "Top floor, where I won't get the traffic so much. I sell shower curtain rings and I just come in from five hundred miles." Luckily my car was turned the right way if they investigated later. One glance had already told me there were only three floors to the place; ten rooms to a floor, five front, five back. "I've got a lot of heavy sleeping to do. I don't want to be disturbed."

The woman wiped her face with a cotton washcloth. "Shower curtain rings, huh?"

"That's right."

"How many nights?" she said in a voice that was nasal and whiney. I wanted to stick a Phillips screwdriver in my ear hole.

"Two, maybe more."

She handed me a key to 313.

The three flights of stairs were narrow, dark and dirty, and so was the corridor at the head of the third flight. A strip of carpet, ground to the semblance of decayed vegetable-matter, all pattern, all color, long erased, adhered to the middle of the hallway, like a form of pollen or fungus encrustation. The smell matched the visual imagery.

I stopped, at the last door there was, and took out a long-shanked iron key. The room was a regular cheap motel room, musty and smelling of old lust, cigarettes, sand, tanning lotion, and stale booze.

A double bed—which used to be brass; you could tell by the bits that glittered here and there over the rusty iron—was nestled against a pink wall with an ugly water stain on the ceiling that resembled Mickey Mouse.

I stripped out of my dusty clothes and fell on the bed; bone-tired, full of pain and ninety-proof and slept for a full fourteen hours.

The next evening a hot, soapy shower turned me almost new again.

I poured myself a drink from a bottle I had picked up in Santa Rita and stood at the window looking across at the ocean. Night was coming through the glass and the sky was turning a burnt orange. I put on a pair of black chinos and a deep blue Hawaiian shirt. I wanted to look like a tourist, but not too much of a tourist.

I went down to the front desk and asked the fat woman if she could give me the names of the popular clubs around the island. For a second she looked at me like I was a pervert, then she reluctantly gave me a list of the most popular.

I started at a place called *The Wave*. It was a huge, high-ceilinged, hanger-type joint where hurrying waitresses kept the drinks coming for all the sailors on leave. The pounding orchestra was almost deafening as mobs of couples did the lindy on the dance floor; pressed together like the ham in a Dagwood sandwich.

I leaned sideways against the bar, scanning the room for any sign of Melissa. I felt old in there, watching the tight young crowd feast upon each other like frenzied fish.

"Come here often, Gramps?" the young, gorgeous-boy bartender asked me.

I took out a fiver from my billfold. "Yeah, it's my favorite place. Come here all the time. Give me a beer."

"Sure you don't want a *Pepto-Bismol?*"

I was getting tired of him.

"No, plain old beer will be fine."

He went to the cooler and took out a bottle of Rheingold. "Fifty cents."

I put the fiver on top of the bar and flashed him Melissa's picture. "Ever see her in here?"

He looked at the picture and shrugged. "Pretty girl. She your daughter?"

My voice came up from my chest with a nasty rumble and I could feel my lip working into a snarl that pulled the corners of my mouth down.

"You're a funny guy," I said. "Regular Milton Berle."

"Who?"

"Never mind. You ever see her in here or not?"

"Or not," he said.

"Would you tell me if you had?"

"Nope."

He took the fiver off the bar.

My eyes felt tight and my lips were pulled back over my teeth. My voice cut into the air and faces turned my way.

"Bring me the change, punk," I told him. He didn't deserve my Lincoln.

I nursed my beer and watched the crowd flitting and dry-humping out on the dance floor.

No Melissa. I finished my beer and left.

Out on the street I breathed in the warm night breeze with the unearthly call of tropical birds and the smell of nicotiana and gardenias sweetening the air.

My first instinct was to pull out my Luckies and light a gasper, but it had been smoky enough in that club and I already smelled like the bottom of an ashtray anyway. It was enough to make me quit smoking for good, but I knew that would never happen.

I roamed the streets and made inquires at lunch-rooms, speakeasies, ten-dollar-a-night flop-houses; conning the bread-lines on North Street, but there was no sight of her.

At the tail end of the night I stopped at a bar on the beach and had a couple more beers and a bucket full of shrimp. I kept my eye out for

Melissa. One or two times I thought I saw a woman who looked like her, but it wasn't.

The next morning I went down to the beach. I picked out a spot under the shade of a massive banyan tree and watched all the pretty girls go by; hoping one of them would be Melissa. The search for her had become an obsession, I knew, but it was more than just getting myself off the hook for Robert's murder, and even more than finding the money. My reasons went farther than that.

♣♣♣

I guess you could call it one of those breaks you get. A call back from the wishing well.

The woman in the gleaming white one-piece swimsuit and the oversized sunglasses was Melissa.

I saw her from a distance crossing the beach on high cork sandals, the long legs tanned the color of honey, smooth and resilient; black hair brushing tan shoulders with the help of a whispery breeze.

It's hard to explain now what I felt that first second I saw her again. I was almost sorry I had found her.

She crossed the street and I moved in behind her on the sun-soaked sidewalk. Men turned to look at her as she passed. Men would always turn to look at her.

Halfway down the block she ducked into the cool green grounds of the *La Playa Resort and Hotel.*

The expensive cabanas she was staying in were at the end of the long walk behind the main hotel.

She turned into the last cabana.

I heard her in there, but I couldn't see inside. All I could do was listen. I heard a fuzzy voice coming through the window:

"Where ya been?"

It was just a murmur. Nothing carried that meant anything:
"The beach."
"I told you we needed to be laying low."
"I know, but I—"
"You never listen, Missy—"
"I know—I know—but I can't stay cooped up in here like a hostage."
"Calm down. It won't be much longer."
Silence.
I listened.
The other voice was closer now:
"I know it's hard, baby."
"It's just...I wasn't made for being cooped up," Melissa said. "I need some action."
Another long silence.
"It's just for a few more days," the other voice said. "We need to make sure the coast is clear. Then we'll take the midnight plane to Frisco. From there we're flying to Strasbourg. We'll lay low for a few months; then it's Australia, Aruba, anywhere you want to go. No one will find us. Ever."
I moved through the brambles under the window sill, and all I got for my pains was a thick mumbling conversation:
"Take your bikini off..."
I listened.
"God, you're so beautiful."
"Careful, baby, they're a little sore."
Another silence.
Then Melissa's voice again:
"Oh my God; where'd you learn how to do that?"
Laughter and the creek of bed springs...

I stood there listening with my hands making fists and the hate pumping through my veins so hard it hurt...

"*Mmmm...*"

More sounds.

"Don't stop."

And heavy breathing.

"That's it. Jesus Christ, that's it! Oh, God. Jesus!"

And a moan.

And a sigh.

More heavy breathing.

And silence.

Chapter Thirty-one

It was then that I knew what I had to do. I was at the precipice and there was no sense delaying the jump any longer.

But before I could do anything I needed a gun. Frank had taken my .38 and finding a new piece wasn't going to be easy, but it wouldn't be impossible either.

I found a hack waiting on the corner and I asked the driver for a fare. He told me to hop in and I told him what I was looking for and that there'd be an extra twenty in it for him.

He didn't even look at me sideways. He told me he was taking me to the South Shore. He told me with a crooked grin that I could find any kind of vice I wanted on the South Shore.

He drove like a maniac, knocking people out of his way. I hung on in the backseat as he barreled down the bustling shore doing a steady sixty-five.

The South Shore of Isle Vista was a place where few tourists dared to venture. Dangling off the Pacific shoreline, its two main drags ran parallel to the water. The cabbie dropped me in front of a shack called the *Spout 'N' Toad* across from the beach. I told him to wait for me. He put the hack in park and kept the meter running.

I went into the Spout 'N' Toad. There was a grilled door and an old Negro behind it who had long ago given up trying to look as if it mattered who came in.

It turned out to be a bucket shop with tables set up on the sides and a long bar running down the middle of the room.

I walked over to the bartender and ordered a tap beer. He drew something that only resembled a beer from a keg and set it down in front of me.

I looked around, made sure no one was within earshot, and told him what I was looking for.

I told him I wanted a piece, one that hadn't done anything except sit in a drawer for the last ten years.

His face had as much expression as a cut of round steak and was about the same color.

He didn't say anything, he just stared at me.

I thought he might be deaf, so I told him again.

He spoke at last, voice thick with expelled smoke.

"Two hundred."

This time it was my turn to give him the staring act.

"One hundred," I said.

His mouth went ugly and his eyes went cold.

"You want that kind of piece, no serial and still in top shape, it's two hundred."

"One-fifty."

He kept his cold black eyes on me, picking me apart. "How do I know you're not a cop?"

"Do I look like a cop?"

"Yeah, you do."

"I'm not a cop."

"One-seventy-five."

"Okay, partner," I said, digging in my pockets for my wallet. I didn't like taking my wallet out in a place like this, but no one seemed to be paying any attention to me anymore.

I handed a hundred and seventy-five dollars across the bar. He slipped it in his pocket and pointed toward a bathroom in the corner of the room.

I stood up and walked into the bathroom. It reeked of urine and stale booze and barfed-up beer smell. I had to hold my breath to avoid retching.

A few seconds later the bartender came in, and without a word he handed me the gat.

It was a .32, with a black rubber grip and a stainless steel finish. I turned it over and looked at the stock. The number had been filed off. I put two fingers over the barrel, held the cocking piece back, twisted the breech block and opened the cylinder. The serial number that was duplicated on the inside of the stock had been filed away as well. I was impressed, most people don't know about the duplicate serial number.

The little gun nestled in my hands like a woman, loaded and fully cocked. Satisfied, I stuck it in the small of my back and got out of there.

♣♣♣

By the time I got back to the *La Playa* it was dark. That was good for what I needed to do.

There was ocean fog in the air and the palm trees dripped with it, leaving them polished and synthetic looking.

I went along the backside of the cabanas beneath a curving line of arc lights that flickered and hissed above me. A storm was brewing on the horizon and the dark palms whispered in the quickening breeze.

I slipped the .32 from the small of my back, checked the action, and pushed off the safety, holding it between thumb and forefinger so that it wouldn't click. The dim light that reflected off the barrel seemed big and nasty.

I could hear the crash of the beach and the wind felt cool against my skin.

I walked on slowly, my shadow moving across the cabana like crawling lava. I went around to the front, the gun held straight out in front of me.

I felt for the knob, twisted it and pushed the door open.

For a while there was nothing but silence, broken finally by the slow ending of a kiss.

It was dark, but I could still see them laid out on the bed like a square root.

Melissa was lying flat on her back, tanned legs glistening in the darkness, her black hair unfurled over the bed like a waterfall with the moon shining off it.

Her eyes were closed and her hands were raised above her head, gripping the iron bars of the headboard.

Every once in a while she would let out a low, quavering moan. I breathed in candle smoke and *Channel* perfume. It was her smell. It filled the air. Her legs were bent slightly and parted. The person between them seemed to be enjoying it almost as much as Melissa was.

My voice was a dull rustle of sound in the darkness. "Hello, Melissa."

She let out a startled gasp and the person between her legs rolled over and stood up quickly.

There are times you want to spit and your mouth goes dry and this was one of those times.

Theresa Kramer stood there, naked as a jay, with her short blonde hair and ripe body. When she saw me her face did tricks until it settled down and then she glowered at me like a dog glowers at the mailman.

Melissa was still in the bed, trying to cover herself with her hands. She looked like a child suddenly roused out of a deep sleep, her lips full and red and bruised looking, eyes half-closed and waiting.

"Elston—"

I held the gun steady on her.

"How did you find us?" she said.

"It took me a long time. It didn't really have to. You don't stay young in my racket very long. I'm not as fast as I used to be. One time I would have had it figured out as soon as I rolled it around a little bit."

We all stood there just staring at each other, me with my gun holding steady, Theresa Kramer looking like she just ate a pigeon, and Melissa on the bed with her lips pressed tight and her nostrils flaring.

"Get out of here!" Theresa Kramer shouted, her voice trembling.

I pointed the gun at her face and told her to shut up.

Her laugh was short and hard. "You're not going to shoot me."

My grin pulled tight at the eyes, compressed across my teeth and stayed that way. "Don't push your luck, sister."

She glared back at me. "You're no more a man than the crabs that slither along the beach."

The ghost of a curl came to my mouth, slightly sardonic. "I'm more of a man than you'll ever pretend to be."

She stood up in a smooth lunge and came at me like a basket of spitting cats. The blow surprised me. Before I could react, she hit me again and my head snapped back.

"She's all I got," Theresa Kramer was screaming. "Don't try to take that away from me!"

I snapped my elbow up under her chin, felt the jarring click of her teeth coming together as she rose up on her toes and shot backwards into the wall, flowing down onto the floor like some thick, slow-running liquid; a heap of blonde hair and long legs.

I turned to Melissa, my face livid with rage, a pulse at my temple beating a tattoo.

She was holding the bed sheets up around her now, in a combination of illogical modesty and legitimate fear.

"Elston—" Her voice had lost its usual scornful stridency and had become little and tinny with fear, like something on a worn-out disk played by a feathered needle.

She made a dive for the door, but I was too quick for her.

I caught her by the hair, whirled her around, and threw her back on the bed.

She sat up, pulled her knees up, hugged them. "I'm sorry, Elston. I never meant for you to get—"

I bit her words off: "Save the Sunday School act, sister; it's over."

The flesh around her neck seemed to get red. Something changed in her eyes and she half twisted her head at me.

"I'll give you all the money, Elston. You can have it all. Whatever's left."

I let my breath out slowly, very slowly. "How much is left?"

"Nine thousand."

"And what the score you made from the heroin you took from Robert's office?"

"Wha—"

"Don't say what heroin, Melissa. I know you sold the heroin on the street, or had someone sell it for you."

Her face wore an almost pitiful expression. I almost felt sorry for her. Almost.

"Another two-fifty," she said; a look like sour milk on her face.

There was a tenseness in my body; a surplus of energy that had been stored away waiting for this moment. I felt it flowing through me, making the skin tighten around my jaws, bunching the muscles in hard knots.

"I really thought I loved you," I told her. "Sounds silly now, doesn't it?"

She turned sweet again and her smile was so unbelievably arousing it'd make the Pope throw down his Bible and grovel at her feet.

"It's not silly, Elston."

My hand holding the gun started to shake a little.

She slithered off the bed and started crawling on the floor toward me. She wasn't trying to hide her nakedness anymore.

"Whatever's left is yours," she said; a slow flush creeping up her throat. "I swear, Elston. You can have it all. It's all yours. We could still run away together, Elston. Like you always wanted. I'd be your girl again. I'd do anything you wanted, I'd let you do whatever you wanted to me. We could go someplace where no one would ever find us. Please...Elston?"

She stood up, so close to me now that one of her black curls brushed my face.

It was all I could do to keep from digging both of my hands in her hair and crushing her with my lips.

"The picture's changed, Melissa," I said instead.

"No, Elston," she breathed, "it's just hanging a little crooked, that's all."

"The money," I said. "Where is it?"

"In the safe."

"Get it!"

She went across the room.

"Slow," I said.

She worked the dial of a small safe in the far wall.

She worked it slowly, turning it back and forth a couple of times. I stood listening to the tumblers click and fall, and then the little round door popped open.

Melissa thrust her arm into the safe.

I raised the gun and pointed it at her shoulder. "You ain't got a piece in there, do you, honey?"

She shook her head.

"Slow," I said again.

Her arm came out holding Robert's black attaché case.

"Empty it," I said.

She held the case upside down and emptied it onto the floor. Stacks of bills flowed out. Stacks and stacks of bills.

I dropped to one knee, touching the money with my left hand, the gun pointed up steadily at her in my right.

I rubbed my hand over the money, the same way I used to run my hands over her.

So this was what it was all about.

Money.

The stuff people never have enough of. Little green pieces of paper crawling with germs that people slave and kill for.

I stood up.

"Put it back in the case," I told her.

She bent down and started putting the stacks of bills back in the case.

"Why'd you do it, Melissa?"

It was like a wave washing up on the beach, then receding back into itself, the way my body was suddenly drained completely dry.

I still wanted her. Goddamn it, I still wanted her.

I leaned forward, put my hand behind her head, and kissed her on the mouth hard.

She licked the saliva off her lips.

I slapped her. Nice and hard. An open-handed slap that left the prints of my fingers across her cheek.

She rubbed her face and tried blinking away the pain.

I slapped her again, harder this time.

It caught her on the side of the face and she fell to her knees at my feet, one hand to her cheek, just her very green eyes looking up at me.

"Let's go back to the beginning," I said. "Tell me how it was done. How did you kill Robert?"

Her eyes were wide and hot as she looked up at me.

"Fuck you."

I reached down and hit her across the face with the back of my hand.

"You're going to tell me how this thing was done if I have to drag you around the room by your hair. Now—how did you kill him?"

Her eyes wreathed into oblique slits, and her lips slashed back, and harsh broken sounds came through. Like rusty laughter. Like laughter left in the rain too long, that has got all mildewed and spoiled.

"You're a fool, Elston. A Goddamn fool," she said crushingly. "We played you like a tambourine. That's right, from the very beginning it was a scam. I never loved you." She laughed again. "You poor lonely fool! How could you ever think I could love you?"

"Why did you kill him?" I said again.

Her steely green eyes glittered with malice. "Vengeance," she said. "He killed my brother."

"Joey Chill," I said.

"I swore I would never let him get away with it. Theresa helped me. We came to Santa Rita together after high school. I love her. I've always loved her. We wanted to run away, but we needed to kill Robert first. We killed him. I snuck up behind him and put a bullet in the back of his head. You were supposed to take the fall for that. At least until we could get away for good."

She let her lips remain parted when she finished speaking. A little flicker of triumph danced in her eyes.

"Why kill Kitty?" I asked her.

"Kitty was just a dumb bump-and-grinder who found out too much. We got rid of a lot when we killed her. No need to give her a kick-back and no need to worry about blackmail in the future. Kitty was a first-class red herring. We figured the cops would pin both murders on you."

I was silent for a little while, and then I said: "Get up."

I took her under the arm and dragged her across the room, swinging her body from side to side like a rag doll. I could feel her legs sweeping bonelessly far over one way, then far back the other way again.

I threw her on top of the bed and looked around the room. Her clothes were scattered on the floor. I took the cotton belt out of her bathrobe and tied one of her hands to the bed. She tried fighting me, but I slapped her on the side of the face. A trickle of blood bubbled over her lower lip.

I couldn't find anything else to tie her other hand with, so I took off my belt, wrapped one end around her wrist and the other to the headboard. She tried biting me and she spit in my face.

I pulled tightly on her restraints until she couldn't move her arms. Then I stood over her, staring down at her naked body as she thrashed on the bed like some kind of wild animal. There were little red bite marks on her nipples and faint blue bruises on the inside of her thighs, love tokens from Theresa Kramer.

I wiped her spit off my face with the back of my hand. "When I'm through with you I'm going to turn you in." It was meant to shake her. It did. "I think they have cells with dirt floors here in Isle Vista. The guards will probably give me the key to the city for handing them something like you. The termites are bad, but they'll keep you company."

She looked up at me. "No one will believe you."

"Yes, they will," I said. "Are you familiar with local ordinances covering private investigators?"

She stared at me blankly.

I smiled. Just a little smile. "When I got to Isle Vista, it was necessary for me to find out whether the local authorities had any reciprocal agreements. It merely consisted of a courtesy call to the local cops. It was a big gamble, but lucky for me they hadn't heard about my problems back in Santa Rita. I was on the run, so I needed them not to have known. Pity for you they didn't."

Her face went white. Cold white sick. Burning-mad crazy-fearful sick.

"The gig is up, honey," I told her. "You're going away for a very long time. The local jakes should be here—" I looked at my wristwatch for effect. "Right about...now."

Like clockwork there was a knock on the door. I smiled.

Melissa screamed and thrashed on the bed. "No, Elston, no!"

A sort of panic twitched in the depths of her eyes.

I picked up the attaché case and went to the door. Melissa was screaming at me to come back. I opened the door and two local Isle Vista plainclothesmen were standing there.

"She's all yours, boys," I said.

The buttons walked in and started reciting the policeman's anthem: "You're under arrest for the murder of Robert Barrett. Anything you say may be used against you in a court of law. You have the right to consult an attorney..."

On my way out I heard Melissa still screaming at me.

It was music to my ears.

Chapter Thirty-two

I was feeling pretty ducky, all things considered. All I had to do now was make a statement in trial court, pay-off half the money to a crooked cop, stash the rest, and then there would be nothing ahead but clear sailing all the way.

Yeah, I was feeling pretty good as I drove back to Santa Rita. The attaché full of cash was sitting right there in the seat next to me. It was a fine traveling companion.

When I got back into town I dropped the Model-T off at Dirty Ernie's, retrieved my old Buick, and drove to my apartment.

It knew I was coming, my apartment; returning home like a hungry runaway.

The place never looked so good.

I went in and poured myself a tall, stiff hooker, took the drink over to my favorite uneasy chair by the window and looked out at the world, watching the dark creep up on it.

The lights of the Chinese restaurant came on, like a satanic moonrise, and I sat there, imagining below me on the street, opium smokers and slant-eyed girls and felt-slippered hirelings of some Fu-Manchu all rushing into that den of Ching Chong pabulum.

"Hello, Elston."

I turned around and saw her standing there in a long yellow rain slicker and fedora, a smoke hanging out the side of her mouth. She had a faraway look in her eye, like she was drinking everything in.

"Do you like kids, Elston?"

I shrugged. "Who's kids?"

Angie's red lipstick parted in a slow smile. "Anybody's kids. Kids."

That night we were awakened suddenly by a noise out in the street. I didn't know what it was at first. Angie had already jumped up from the bed, naked as a pole-dancing nurse.

"What's going on out there?" I asked sleepily.

Then I heard four explosions that rattled the panes of the window.

"That's mortar fire," I said. "It's got to be coming from the Bay."

Suddenly, there were several more explosions, and then popping noises that sounded like gunfire cracking through the air.

"Maybe the war's come to Santa Rita," Angie said.

I started to say something, but the sound of people cheering, car horns blowing, and church bells ringing drowned out my words.

I jumped out of bed and joined Angie at the window. Down below, the street was beginning to fill with people.

Someone in the crowded street yelled, "*Hirohito's surrendered!*"

Another person cried, "*The war is over!*"

Hundreds of people filled the street and sidewalks. They were laughing and hugging and kissing and cheering. Some were still in their nightclothes. They were beating pie tins and pots and pans. Firecrackers popped around them.

"I can't believe it," Angie said. "The war is over."

I put my arm around her sun-freckled shoulder and told her to come back to bed.

THE END

Jason Holscher grew up in Minneapolis spying on his neighbors and taking notes in a little black book. He currently resides in a fortified compound on the banks of the Cannon River.

CPSIA information can be obtained at www.ICGtesting.com
Printed in the USA
243040LV00001B/18/P